The Scramble

Also From Kristen Proby

Blush For Me
The Beauty of Us
Savor You

The Boudreaux Series:
Easy Love
Easy Charm
Easy Melody
Easy Kisses
Easy Magic
Easy Fortune
Easy Nights

The With Me In Seattle Series:
Come Away With Me
Under the Mistletoe With Me
Fight With Me
Play With Me
Rock With Me
Safe With Me
Tied With Me
Burn With Me
Breathe With Me
Forever With Me
Stay With Me
Indulge With Me
Love With Me
Dance With Me
Dream With Me
You Belong With Me
Imagine With Me
Escape With Me
Flirt With Me
Take a Chance With Me

Huckleberry Bay:
Lighthouse Way
Fernhill Lane

The Scramble

A Single in Seattle Novella

By Kristen Proby

1001 DARK NIGHTS
PRESS

The Scramble
A Single in Seattle Novella
By Kristen Proby

1001 Dark Nights
Copyright 2022 Kristen Proby
ISBN: 979-8-88542-007-5

Foreword: Copyright 2014 M. J. Rose

Published by 1001 Dark Nights Press, an imprint of Evil Eye
Concepts, Incorporated

Sign up for the 1001 Dark Nights Newsletter
and be entered to win a Tiffany Key necklace.

There's a contest every month!

Go to www.1001DarkNights.com to subscribe.

**As a bonus, all subscribers can download FIVE FREE exclusive
books!**

Acknowledgments from the Author

I would like to thank Liz Berry, MJ Rose, Jillian Stein and the entire team at 1001 Dark Nights for including me once more in this year's novella line up, and for always making me feel like I'm part of your family. I love you all!

One Thousand and One Dark Nights

Once upon a time, in the future...

*I was a student fascinated with stories and learning.
I studied philosophy, poetry, history, the occult, and
the art and science of love and magic. I had a vast
library at my father's home and collected thousands
of volumes of fantastic tales.*

*I learned all about ancient races and bygone
times. About myths and legends and dreams of all
people through the millennium. And the more I read
the stronger my imagination grew until I discovered
that I was able to travel into the stories... to actually
become part of them.*

*I wish I could say that I listened to my teacher
and respected my gift, as I ought to have. If I had, I
would not be telling you this tale now.
But I was foolhardy and confused, showing off
with bravery.*

*One afternoon, curious about the myth of the
Arabian Nights, I traveled back to ancient Persia to
see for myself if it was true that every day Shahryar
(Persian: شهریار, "king") married a new virgin, and then
sent yesterday's wife to be beheaded. It was written
and I had read that by the time he met Scheherazade,
the vizier's daughter, he'd killed one thousand
women.*

Something went wrong with my efforts. I arrived in the midst of the story and somehow exchanged places with Scheherazade — a phenomena that had never occurred before and that still to this day, I cannot explain.

Now I am trapped in that ancient past. I have taken on Scheherazade's life and the only way I can protect myself and stay alive is to do what she did to protect herself and stay alive.

Every night the King calls for me and listens as I spin tales. And when the evening ends and dawn breaks, I stop at a point that leaves him breathless and yearning for more. And so the King spares my life for one more day, so that he might hear the rest of my dark tale.

As soon as I finish a story... I begin a new one... like the one that you, dear reader, have before you now.

Prologue

Maddie
Fifteen Years Ago…

"I don't want to go to the football game." I cross my arms over my chest and glare at my dad, who just sighs and gives me the look that says I'm going to lose this argument. "I have homework to do, and I'm pulling extra work for college prep. I don't have time to go watch a stupid game."

"It's homecoming," Dad says sternly. "And your sister is cheering in it. She'd like for us to be there."

"She's up for Homecoming Queen," Mom adds. "We should all be there to support her."

"I support her. I hope she gets it. She looks great in the dress she chose, and she's totally awesome and popular, so she'll win. Blah blah blah. I don't have to be there for her to be crowned. I have so much to do here."

They shake their heads at me, but they don't understand. I *like* to study. I like to work hard, and I don't have the time or inclination to *play*.

People at school make fun of me because I'm a nerd, but I don't care. I like being a nerd.

And some people think it's stupid that I love math. They think wanting to be an accountant is boring.

But it's not boring. I have a family *full* of people with exciting careers. Hell, my uncle is a professional football player, and another is a rock star.

I don't need flashy. I don't need to perform.

I *like* boring.

"You're going," Dad says. "You can take one night off from homework. I can't believe I have to force my kid *not* to do schoolwork."

"You can't make me," I fire back, surprising us all. "You're not my real dad anyway. If I want to stay home and do absolutely *nothing*, that's my choice."

"*Madeline Rose Montgomery*," Mom says in surprise.

Dad just blinks at me and then turns away. But I can see that I hurt his feelings.

"I'm sorry," I say immediately and rush to him. I launch myself into his arms and hug him so tight I fear I might pop his head off. "I'm really sorry. You're my dad. I'm just so frustrated. I don't want to go to the game."

"Why?" His voice is soft now, like he's not mad anymore, just confused. "Why don't you want to go, Buttercup?"

"I don't fit in there. Kids don't like me. I'm not fun enough. I don't find them funny, and I just want to work."

"You're going to have your whole life to work. Trust me on that." He sets me on my feet and kisses the tip of my nose like he's done since I was a little kid when he came into our lives. "Besides, you won't be there alone. Your mom and I will be there, too. So will Drew."

"Great. Now I'm the nerd who has to sit with her parents because she doesn't have any friends."

"You have friends," Mom insists.

"None of them are going to the football game," I mutter, not bothering to tell them that, aside from Josie, I really *don't* have any friends. Not close ones, anyway.

And that's okay because high school kids are dumb.

"If it means that much to you, I'll go." I sigh and turn toward the bedroom so I can grab my stuff. "But after halftime, when we know if Josie won, I'm coming home."

"Deal," Dad says with a grin.

When I leave the room, I hear them talking about me. They're worried because I work too hard and don't have enough fun.

But work *is* fun.

No one else seems to get that.

Chapter One

Maddie
Present Day

I take off my reading glasses and rub my tired eyes. I'm only an hour into the eight-hour flight from Seattle to Reykjavík, Iceland, on Christmas Eve, and I've been working every minute of it.

A signal chimes in my ear, and I open my eyes to glance down at my laptop. A message pops up from my sister.

Josie: *Tell me you're in the air.*

I grin and type.

Me: *An hour in. I land early, around six. Why am I going to Iceland again?*

The bubbles jump as my twin replies, and I sip from the bottle of water the flight attendant gave me. They've also served dinner and dessert.

First class is the only way to go when flying internationally.

Josie: *Because it's Christmas, and the whole fam is here. Don't be a baby. It's so pretty. Get here FASTER!*

Me: *I'm not the pilot. I'll come wake you up when I get there. Get some sleep!*

I sigh and rub my eyes once more. It's been the week from absolute hell. If there's a darker place than hell, that's what it's been.

The end of the month is always bad when it comes to my job, but add in the end of the *year*, and I'm swamped. I really don't have time to fly halfway around the world for a holiday. I tried to get out of it, but my uncle Luke came to my house himself and talked me into going.

He's one of my favorite people. How could I turn him down?

I couldn't.

So now, instead of being in my office like I should be, I'm on an airplane, soaring over the polar ice cap on my way to meet up with my entire family in Iceland.

Sometimes, my life is weird.

"That's the third time you've sighed in five minutes."

I frown and look around. Suddenly, the wall separating me from the first-class pod next to me lowers, and the greenest eyes I've ever seen smile over at me.

"What?"

Great comeback, Mad. Why am I so damn awkward with men? With people in general? I didn't used to be when I was little.

But the older I got, the more awkward I became.

I like to blame it on hormones.

"You. Sighing." He shifts so he can look at me closer. "Why so down, beautiful?"

I feel my cheeks flush and stare at my laptop.

I don't think anyone, aside from my dad and other family members, has ever called me beautiful.

"I'm not down. I'm busy."

"Ah. So, going on a business trip, then?" He nods. "Me, too."

"It's not a business trip. I'm meeting my family in Reykjavík for Christmas."

I glance over, and his eyebrows climb. "It's Christmas in…wait, I have to do math with the time change." He mimics doing math in the air with his finger. "Carry the one…now. It's Christmas there *now.*"

"I know." I sigh again, and he smiles. Holy shit, that smile. Why is he so…*hot?* His teeth aren't completely straight, but that smile just made my lady bits stand up and do the cha-cha.

"I'm Dylan." He awkwardly offers me his hand over the panel between us. "And you are?"

"Late." I try to ignore the awareness that crawls up my arm from his touch. "I'm late, and I *hate* being late."

"So, why are you?" He leans on his elbow, propping his chin in his hand to give me his undivided attention.

It's a little disconcerting.

I shake my head and close the laptop, resigning myself to the fact that I'm taking a break I really can't afford. Yet I'm not totally annoyed by this guy, so I might as well chat with him.

"I couldn't get away until today. To be honest, I should be in the office all week. But my uncle Luke talked me into going to Iceland with the rest of the family."

"Oh, it's an extended-family thing. How many people are going?"

I blink at him. "A few dozen, probably."

"I'm sorry, what?"

"It's a big family." I shrug. "I don't know why I felt obligated. It's not like they'd really miss me with all those people there."

"I bet they would." His eyes narrow on me. "Miss you, I mean."

"Why are you going to Iceland?" I change the subject, not sure what to do with all the flirtation from a sexy stranger on a freaking *airplane.*

"Work, like I said."

"What do you do?"

Those green eyes smile at me again. If I were a romantic person, I'd say I could lose myself in them.

They're like the mossy hills of Ireland.

Not that I've ever *been* to Ireland. We have family there, but I've never gotten the chance to go.

"I'm a travel writer for a major network."

"No way."

He laughs, and I feel it all the way to my toes. "Way. They send me all over the world to scout things, do some writing, and then they send in crews to film."

"Wow, that sounds exciting."

"What about you?"

I frown. "What about me?"

"What do *you* do that you couldn't get away for a family vacation to one of the most beautiful places in the world?"

"Oh, that. I'm an accountant."

I expect him to balk and ask me why I would choose something so *boring.* That's usually the response I get.

But he just nods slowly. "Wow, that's kind of cool."

I stare at him for a full ten seconds and then burst out laughing. I laugh until my sides hurt. I haven't laughed this hard in years.

When I slow down and wipe a tear from my eye, he passes me a tissue.

"No one has *ever* said that what I do is cool."

"Hey, aside from figuring out time zones because I'm an expert at that these days, I'm not good with numbers. So, meeting someone who is *is* cool."

"Thanks." I wipe the last of the tears and take a deep breath.

"What's your name?"

"Oh, sorry. Maddie. Maddie Montgomery. And I really should get back to work." I point at the laptop.

"I hate to break it to you, Maddie Montgomery, but you're on vacation. Therefore, you absolutely should *not* work."

"Yeah, well, my clients would disagree with you."

"Do your clients never take holidays?"

"Oh, they do. And then they try to write them off on their taxes." I grin at him. "Sometimes, they can. But most of the time, they can't."

"Can you write this one off?" he asks.

"No." I shake my head.

"What if I asked you accounting questions?"

"I could only write it off if you actually hired me, and there was work to be done in Iceland. Nice try, though. Besides, I'm not paying for it. Uncle Luke treated all of us cousins for Christmas."

"I like Uncle Luke," Dylan says with a laugh.

"You probably do," I say with a nod. "He's Luke Williams."

The smile falls from Dylan's face. "The movie guy?"

"That's him."

"He did a guest spot on our channel a few years ago. Narrated a limited series for us."

"Really? I didn't know that."

"Small world," he murmurs. "So, tell me, Maddie…"

Here it comes. The part where a guy just wants all the information about my family and doesn't give a rat's ass about me. Why did I tell him who Luke is? Why couldn't I just flirt with a guy without making it weird?

"What's that?"

"What do you have planned while you're in Iceland?"

"Nothing." I reopen the computer. "I'm only there for about twenty-four hours. Then, I'm headed back home."

"Oh, fuck that."

My head whips around, and I stare at him.

"Excuse me?"

"You're flying all the way to Iceland, one of the most magical places in the freaking world, and you're not going to see *anything*?"

I hold up the computer and give it a little wave. "Work."

"Nope. No work. Take the week and enjoy it, Maddie. You only get this one life. Live a little."

"I appreciate your concern, but you don't even know me, Dylan."

"I'd like to, if I'm being honest. I took one look at you when I boarded and just knew."

"Knew what?" Why is my heart suddenly beating so damn fast?

He leans a little closer, and I catch the scent of cedar mixed with something spicy.

"I knew that I wanted to know you."

"Why?"

Those green eyes narrow, and something else replaces the humor in them. Heat? Lust?

Whatever it is, it makes the cha-cha turn into the merengue.

"Sexy woman, wearing glasses. Have I mentioned that I have a thing for glasses?"

"No."

"Well, I do. Your fingers are long and slim and fly over that keyboard. It's sexy."

"My *typing* is sexy?"

"Hmm." He nods slowly. "And I like the scarf you're wearing."

I glance down at the red silk scarf with white cats on it that Josie got me for Christmas *last* year.

"The red makes your eyes look like pools of melted chocolate."

"Um, am I in an alternate universe?" I glance around to find the other passengers in first class completely ignoring us—watching screens, snacking, or sleeping.

And then the overhead lights go out, casting the cabin into darkness so the passengers who want to sleep the night away until we land can do so.

"Mood lighting," Dylan whispers next to me, and I giggle. "I'm breaking through that shell of yours."

"I think you're just wearing me down."

"Same difference."

He touches me, and I think my heart might explode. Then he reaches over and tucks my hair behind my ear.

"There, now I can see your face better."

"Do you do this on every flight, Dylan?"

He raises an eyebrow.

"You know, flirt with the girl next to you so shamelessly she invites you to do her in the bathroom?"

He bites his lip and then laughs, and I suddenly feel so stupid. I wish the floor of the plane would open and send me down into Alaska.

"First of all, no. I usually avoid talking to people on planes like the plague. And number two, did you just invite me to the bathroom?"

Did I?

I start to shake my head and then reconsider.

I set my laptop in its bag at my feet, unbuckle the seatbelt, and with a small smile at Dylan, stand and walk in the darkness to the bathroom.

What am I doing? I never, ever, *ever* do stuff like this. The last time I'd had sex, we had a different president.

I'm not promiscuous.

But damn if he's not sexy and charming and—

Before I can complete the thought, the door opens, and Dylan slips inside, locking the door.

We're so smooshed together I have no idea how this will work.

"Not much room in here," I whisper, not wanting anyone to hear us.

Not that they could over the sound of the plane, but still.

"We don't need much room."

I fist my hands in the front of his shirt, partly so I don't fall backward, and partly because I want to get my hands on him.

"Maddie, if you aren't sure about this, I'll leave right now."

My breath comes fast, and I can't take my eyes off his lips. Damn, I want him to kiss me more than I've ever wanted anything in my life.

"Are you ever going to kiss me?"

Those lips twitch.

"I don't have a condom with me, Maddie. I didn't plan this."

"Hell, who does?" I glance up into laughing green eyes. "Okay, don't answer that."

"So, we're going to have to get inventive."

I've never been inventive when it comes to sex. I'm a typical missionary-with-the-lights-out kind of girl.

This is definitely *not* that.

"Uh, sure. Okay."

He tips up my chin and hovers his lips over mine. He's *inches* away, just waiting.

For what? I have no idea.

"Melted chocolate," he whispers before finally covering my mouth with his and sinking into me. It starts out soft and sweet, so new that it takes my breath away.

Then, his hands cup my face.

He groans a little, the appreciative sound deep in his throat.

I suddenly can't handle it anymore. I plunge my fingers into his thick, dark hair, and he cups my ass, lifting me until I fit around him.

"Gotta be fast," he warns. "Otherwise, someone will come knocking."

"Fast," I agree as he braces me on the tiny excuse for a sink, and I reach for his jeans.

"Hop up."

I lift my ass, and he wiggles my leggings down over my hips, his lips never leaving mine.

He growls when I set him free and cup his hard length in my hand.

"Ah, shit."

"You're *very* hard."

"From the minute I saw you," he confirms. "I'd like to look at you when I do this, but there's no space."

"Just do it."

Have I ever wanted someone so much? No. Never. I want him inside me so badly I'm ready to beg for it.

He turns me around and bends me over just a bit. The next thing I know, he's rubbing his fingers over and into me.

"So fucking wet," he says against my ear.

"In me," I breathe.

That's all the invitation he needs.

He fills me completely, and with his hands braced on either side of me, fucks me hard and fast, making me come just as hard and fast.

When he's ready to come, he jerks away, opens the toilet, and finishes into it.

"Wow, good aim." I'm out of breath, watching as he milks himself dry. I'll be damned if I don't want him all over again.

But I know that's not possible.

Dylan tucks himself away, straightens his shirt, and then kisses me hard before walking out of the tiny restroom.

I lock the door behind him, clean myself up, and then stare at my reflection in the mirror.

"What in the actual fuck, Maddie?"

Chapter Two

Dylan

My body is still humming when I take my seat and pull in a long, deep breath.

I can honestly say that was a first for me, and I didn't think there were many firsts left out there to experience.

Maddie returns to her seat a few moments later, and after a quick glance around, it's obvious no one else in the cabin is aware that we just fucked in the restroom.

"I'm going to call you," I inform her after she fastens her seatbelt and readjusts that sexy little scarf.

"What are you going to call me?" She grins at her joke. I want to yank her over the barrier and onto my lap so I can enjoy her all over again.

"Send me your number."

She frowns at me. "I don't have *your* number. Besides, we're on a plane with no cell service."

"Hmm, you're right. We'll take care of it when we land then. Because I have every intention of seeing you in Iceland."

"I'm only there for one day," she reminds me.

"I'll talk you out of that, too."

"Do you always get what you want?"

I tilt my head to the side, thinking it over. "Pretty much. The important things, anyway. And I've decided that this is *very* important."

She flushes again and casts her gaze down. Jesus, she's beautiful.

Has no one ever told her that before? I find that hard to believe.

"I do have work to do, though. Where are you staying?" I offer her some Twizzlers. She takes one and bites into it.

"At some resort with blue water."

"Blue Lagoon." I nod and nibble my Twizzler. "I'm staying there, too. It's the nicest place in the country, although there are some really nice bed and breakfasts here and there."

"How many times have you been?" she asks.

"Nine. No, this is my ninth."

"Nine times? Wow, you must really like it."

"It's spectacular. Especially this time of year. It's dark and cold, so not many people travel to Iceland now. So, it's quiet. And the northern lights are just amazing."

That makes her eyes light up, and I make a vow to myself, here and now, that I'll make love to her under the aurora borealis.

As soon and as often as possible.

"Maybe that's why Luke chose this time of year to bring us all there," Maddie muses. "Because this was the only time he could manage to reserve the majority of the resort for everybody."

"That could be." I want to touch her again, but the stupid divider between us makes it awkward. Instead, I cross my arms over my chest and watch as Maddie yawns. "You should get some sleep."

"I really do have to work." She blinks slowly, her eyes clearly heavy. "But maybe a short nap won't hurt."

She reclines her seat until she's almost lying down and tucks the pillow from the airline under her head.

I'm not sure I know what I'm doing. I'm on this trip to work, not to get distracted by the sexiest woman I've ever seen.

Yet it looks like that's how it's going to go.

Because I'm absolutely not going to deprive myself of her. Not for anything.

* * * *

Once we landed, I talked Maddie into sharing a car with me. After arriving at the resort, I helped her to her room before going in search of mine. But I couldn't sleep. Thanks to jet lag, I never slept well after landing in foreign countries, so I decided to lose myself in some work.

I like to document the flight time, the ease in which I was able to get to my destination, and what I thought of the airline. Then I do the same with the resort.

I jot down some thoughts about the ride from the airport.

I don't mention the sexual tension that bounced between Maddie and me like a ping-pong ball.

I don't think my boss would appreciate that added narrative.

But now, several hours later, I decide to walk around the resort and interview some staff. It's Christmas, but the hotel will still have staff available for the guests. It's mid-morning, but the sun hasn't risen yet for the day, and all the lights hung for the holidays sparkle as I walk through the lobby to the desk.

"Can I help you?"

Before I can answer, I see Maddie out of the corner of my eye.

"Sorry, just a second."

I step away to watch her. She's walking with another woman who looks a *lot* like her, and two younger-looking men. They're all laughing as they walk into the restaurant with its gourmet breakfast spread for the guests to enjoy.

I walk in behind them, watching as they load up plates and then fill a small booth against the windows that frames the gorgeous waters of the blue lagoon.

Maddie looks around, her brown eyes wide as she takes it all in. Her lips move, and although I can't hear her, I can see what she says.

This is amazing.

I decide to shoot her a text.

Me: *You look well rested.*

She pulls her phone out of her pocket, reads the text, and then scans the room until she finds me.

She doesn't smile, she simply looks down at her phone and replies.

Maddie: *I got a couple of hours. You?*

Me: *No. Kept thinking about you.*

I glance up in time to see the woman I assume is her sister looking over her shoulder before peppering Maddie with questions.

The sister's eyes find me, and she grins, bumps Maddie's shoulder, and then steals her sister's phone, tapping vigorously.

Maddie: *Come join us!*

Without replying, I walk to the table. With my eyes pinned to

Maddie, I smile. "Good morning."

"Hi," she says. "This is my sister, Josie, my brother, Drew, and our cousin, Keaton."

"Nice to meet you." I nod at each of them, then return my attention to the gorgeous woman I just met yet feel as if I've known for years.

"You should sit," Josie says as she slides out of the booth, making room for me next to Maddie. Then, she climbs back in, effectively trapping me. "So, you met on the plane?"

"We did," Maddie confirms. "Dylan is here on business."

"What kind of business?" Drew wants to know. "Besides hitting on women on airplanes."

"Actually, I don't think I've ever done that before." I steal some fruit from Maddie's plate and fill the others in on what I do for a living and why I'm in Iceland. "What about the rest of you?"

"I'm a nurse," Josie says with a smile. "Keaton restores cars, and Drew plays for a living."

"I'm a fucking *coach*," Drew says with a scowl. "I don't *play*."

"It's kind of the same thing," Maddie adds but reaches over to pat her brother on the shoulder. "But if it makes you feel any better, you're really good at it."

"So, are you saying that Uncle Will just *played* for a living?" Drew demands.

"No, he kicked ass," Josie replies.

"Wait, who's Uncle Will?" I ask.

"Will Montgomery," Maddie says with a shrug. "Have you heard of him?"

I swallow hard and keep the fact that I had posters of the man on my wall when I was a kid to myself.

"Yeah, I've heard of him."

"Anyway, we got off on a tangent," Josie says. "We've been trying to talk Maddie into staying for the week. The rest of us are here through New Year's, but she thinks she has to run back home to work."

"I *do* have to work," Maddie insists, and I can see from the look in her eyes that she's nervous about the job.

"Maybe you can compromise," I suggest. "Since you brought your laptop, set aside a few hours each morning for work, then enjoy the rest of your vacation."

"A working vacation," Josie agrees with a smile. "You have to admit, that's a good idea."

"You need the time, Mads." Keaton's the quietest of the bunch, but Maddie nods at his words, seeming to let them soak in. "You deserve it, too—just like the rest of us."

"My boss isn't thrilled that I came," she admits softly. "It's not a great time for me to take a vacation."

"How many have you taken since you started that job eight years ago?" Josie asks but answers before her sister can. "*Zero.* The big nada. So, if he has an issue with this trip, he can kiss your fine ass."

"It really *is* a fine ass," I agree, turning everyone's attention to me.

"Don't make us beat the shit out of you on Christmas, dude," Drew says. "You can't just say shit like that about my sister right to my face."

"Sure, I can." I smile at him and then turn my attention back to Maddie. "It's the truth. I'd also like it if you stayed."

"You can't spend *all* your time with the family," Josie says, nudging her sister once more. "Say you'll stay. You know you want to."

"Okay." Maddie takes a deep breath as if that were the most difficult word she's ever uttered. "I'll stay. Of course, I didn't bring enough clothes for the whole week. I only packed for a day or two."

"Please." Josie rolls her eyes. "You know the rest of us girls overpacked. We've got you and every other woman in this resort covered for a month."

"That's not an exaggeration," Keaton says to me. "Not even close."

* * * *

With Maddie off enjoying the holiday with her family, I head back to my room to get ahead on my work. Now that I know she'll be here all week, I want to make sure I can spend as much time with her as possible.

I'm in the middle of writing a paragraph and considering placing an order with room service when my phone rings.

"Merry Christmas, Mom."

"You know, I find it funny that you were in Seattle just yesterday and couldn't stay long enough to spend the holiday with your mother."

I wince and sit back in the chair. "You know I needed to experience Christmas at this resort for the channel."

"You likely could have gone tomorrow and seen all the same things, but we've had this argument at least three times this month, so I'll stop for now."

"Try six times."

"Your father sends his love. He's napping in his chair."

I grin, thinking of my parents. They're the best. Though I don't remember the last time I spent the holidays with them.

Next year, I'll be there. I won't leave for a scouting mission until after the first of January.

Probably.

"Your aunt Suzie and her family are coming over later," Mom says, filling me in on what's happening for the festivities at their house later today. I haven't seen Aunt Suzie in years. "What will you have to eat?"

"I don't know, whatever sounds good from the room service menu."

And maybe a certain brunette later.

But I leave that part out. If I even so much as breathe a syllable about a woman, Mom will hound me for days.

She's desperate for me to marry and give her grandkids.

"How long are you there again?" she asks.

"Through the first. Maybe a little longer. We'll see. There are parts of Iceland I haven't seen before, and I'd like to catch them this time since I'm here."

"That makes sense. Just be careful out there. It's dark and cold. Icy."

"I'll be fine. The dark doesn't bother me. Really. And we should be able to see the northern lights every night."

"We?" I can almost see her sit up straighter in her chair, cradling the phone to her cheek harder. "Who's *we*, Dylan?"

"Figure of speech, Mom. You know, *we*, as in everyone in Iceland."

She blows out a breath. "Well, damn."

Chapter Three

Maddie

"So, where are we having family Christmas in this place?" I unpack the few things I brought with me as Josie tucks a pillow under her chest while lying on the bed, watching me as I bustle about the room.

"Uncle Luke rented out an awesome suite on the top floor. It's two stories and has its own lagoon. The presents and stuff will be in there."

"This *is* the present," I reply in surprise.

"Oh, I agree. But, apparently, there's a little more because all the parents agreed that we must have *something* to open on Christmas morning. As if we're all toddlers."

"Huh." I shake my head. "I didn't bring presents for anyone, Jos."

"Don't worry about it. You always stress about this stuff, and it's literally *fine*."

"Where's Brax?"

Brax is Josie's musician boyfriend. They were together for a few years and broke up. Now, they're back together again.

"He's sleeping. Jet lag sucks. We're not meeting with the family until three anyway."

I nod. Once I've put away the last of my toiletries, I crash in the chair by the window with an awesome view of the lava fields.

"The sun is starting to come up."

"We only have about five hours of daylight here." Josie rolls onto her side and looks out the windows. "Surprisingly, I don't hate it.

Maybe it's because Seattle has so many dark, rainy days."

"Maybe it's because you're used to working the night shift at the hospital."

She smiles. "Probably. Okay, enough small talk. Tell me *everything* about Dylan."

My stomach knots. I usually tell Josie *everything*. I think it's a twin rule or something. But I don't know how she'll react to learning what I did on that airplane.

"I don't know much about him," I reply and yawn, trying to be nonchalant.

"Bullshit."

I sigh, rub my hands over my clean face, and then look at my sister, who's watching me with shrewd eyes.

"You know him. Because no one who doesn't *know* a woman looks at her the way he looked at you this morning."

"Okay, this is going to be the craziest story I've ever told you, and you can't tell the cousins."

She blinks at me in surprise. "All right. Give it to me."

"I didn't know him until I got on that airplane. And then we fucked in the bathroom."

She just keeps blinking. "On the *airplane*?"

"Yes."

I chew my bottom lip, waiting for her response.

"I know people talk about it all the time but is that even *possible*? I mean, they're so small."

"You don't need much room." I smile to myself, hearing Dylan's words echoing in my head.

"Oh, I like that smile." She sits up, crosses her legs, and then hugs the pillow to her chest. "I like it a *lot*. That's a satisfied smile."

"Yeah, well, it was fun."

"Did you just say *fun*?"

"If you say a *word* about me not being fun, I'll come over there and break your nose."

"You always were violent. I'd say you got it from Dad, but despite being a former SEAL, he might be the gentlest human alive. Okay, so, there were airplane shenanigans."

"Yes."

"What else?"

"He just flirted with me, practically the whole flight. And he's *nice*. Which is weird."

"I know they seem to be fewer and fewer these days, but there *are* nice guys out there."

"Yeah, well, we seem to be related to ninety percent of them. Anyway, I don't know much about Dylan other than what he does for a living and that the sex is beyond anything I've ever had before."

"Honey, as a woman well into her thirties, it's about damn time. I'm glad we talked you into staying the week. Now, you can hang out with Dylan more. Have a vacation fling. If that's all it is, it's still time well spent."

"Huh. I never considered a vacation fling."

"Well, I say *start* considering it." She glances at the clock. "We should get up to Luke and Nat's suite."

"I need to put on a little makeup. Just a smidge so I don't look like a jet-lagged zombie."

"Hurry. I'll text Brax and make sure he's up."

She grabs for her phone, and I hurry into the bathroom to put on a little mascara, a bit of under-eye concealer, and some lip gloss. I'm no fashion plate, but it's a small improvement.

"Brax will meet us up there," Josie announces when I join her. "Wait until you see this suite, Mad. You won't believe it."

We walk down the hall to the elevator and swipe a key card for the penthouse. According to Josie, all the family's cards work for the fancy suite level.

When we arrive, my mouth drops.

This isn't just a hotel suite. This is an experience.

It's a two-floor apartment with a massive living room, and it looks like Luke had extra couches and chairs brought in for seating.

The biggest Christmas tree I've ever seen stands in front of the huge wall of windows—it must be at least twenty feet tall.

"Holy hell." I don't bother to whisper. Suddenly, everyone realizes I'm here and swarms me with hugs and kisses.

"You're here," Mama says as she plants one on my cheek. "Did you get any rest?"

"A little. Wow, this is something. They really *do* have their own private lagoon out there."

"We're all going to swim later," Olivia informs me before pulling me in for a hug. "Thank you for coming, even though I know you didn't really want to. It wouldn't have been the same without you."

"Don't make me cry on Christmas."

She laughs as the door opens once more, and Brax walks inside, joining Josie.

It looks like everyone is here, all packed into the suite. Some are in the living room, others upstairs in the loft.

A few people sit on the stairs, chatting.

I even see the grandparents sitting at a large dining room table with coffee and pastries laid out before them.

Grandpa Steven sends me a wink.

Despite the size of the suite, there are so many of us that we pack it almost to bursting. But no one cares.

We just love being together. And, I didn't think anyone would really notice that I wasn't here, but as usual, I'm reminded that that's not the case.

We're all well-loved.

"Attention, everyone," Uncle Luke says, tapping his coffee mug with a spoon. He's so handsome in his simple long-sleeved red Henley and jeans. He looks like a movie star despite his casual appearance. "I just want to say thank you for coming."

He looks directly at me and smiles.

"I know it wasn't convenient for all of you, but we appreciate you taking the time to travel all this way. We have a few excursions planned this week, and you're welcome to do as much or as little as you want. Although I recommend snowmobiling on the glacier. You just can't do that every day."

"We have gifts," Natalie adds, wrapping her arm around Luke's waist as he loops his across her shoulders. They stand as one unit, the way they have for pretty much as long as I can remember. "They're not extravagant, but everyone should have a little something to open on Christmas morning."

"Why such spoiling this year?" The question comes from Stella, who's sitting on the couch with her boyfriend, Gray. "I mean, you guys always do too much at the holidays, but this is a lot, even for you."

Luke takes a breath, thinking it over, and then shrugs a shoulder. "Because you're all, well, mostly adults. Those who aren't quite there yet are close. Our parents are still with us, and I don't want to sound morose or be a downer, but it won't always be this way. I have a feeling life is about to change, and we all wanted this moment before that really starts to happen."

"Well, shit. Now I'm crying," Erin says, wiping a tear from her cheek. Her daddy, Will, leans in to kiss her head.

"Finn and Emma are the youngest, and they're in high school," my aunt Jules reminds us all. "So, yeah, this is a special time in our family."

"I'd like to make it a little more special," Gray says as he kisses Stella's hand and gets on one knee in front of her.

The room hushes in surprise. I glance at Stella's dad, Nate, and am surprised when I don't see his eyes flash and hands fist. Instead, he just reaches for his wife's hand, and Jules' eyes tear up.

"Stella McKenna, you are the best thing that's ever come into my life. You are a force to be reckoned with."

"Hell yes, she is," someone calls out, making us all smile.

"You also have the kindest heart and a work ethic that inspires me every day. I love you so much it steals the breath from my lungs, and I know that if I don't make you mine, I'll regret it for the rest of my life.

"So, I'm asking you here, in front of every single person who means the most to you, and in the most terrifying way I can think of—"

There's laughter now.

"Will you do me the honor of marrying me?"

"Oh my God, yes! Of course, I will."

"This calls for celebratory mimosas," Olivia announces, and *her* fiancé, the one and only Vaughn Barrymore, kisses her squarely on the mouth.

Uncle Luke is right. Our family is changing. Growing. And it won't always look like this: so simple—if that word can even be used to describe our family.

I'm so, *so* glad that I came for this. I wouldn't have wanted to miss it for the world.

* * * *

"All the cousins are putting on the Christmas pajamas we got this morning and going to the conference room where the movie theater is set up," Haley informs me after we've all had food and opened presents. "I think it's going to be a double feature. *It's a Wonderful Life* and *White Christmas.*"

"Okay. I'm heading down to my room for a bit, but I'll catch most of it."

"You can always nap during the movie," she suggests with a wink.

Despite being more than a decade younger than me, Haley and I are close. We don't have anything at all in common, but that doesn't matter.

So, I promise to come back up after I put some stuff away and change into the green pajamas that say *Ho Ho Ho* in red all over them.

Before I can leave my room, I get a text from Dylan.

My stomach does a little twirl in anticipation as I open it.

Dylan: *How is your day going?*

Me: *So far so good. How about you?*

I bite my lip and sit in my chair while waiting for his reply. Finally, his message pops up.

Dylan: *It started amazing, then went a little flat. But it's going to start looking up.*

Me: *Oh? How so?*

Dylan: *You're going to come to my room for a while.*

I laugh and remember that I'm supposed to watch Christmas movies with my cousins. I could *probably* make an excuse for why I was even later than I told Haley. And *It's a Wonderful Life* is a long movie, isn't it?

It always seems like it.

Deciding to fit both into my afternoon, I text him back.

Me: *What room number?*

Dylan: *4067*

He's just down the hall from me. I slide my feet into my slippers and, remembering the key to the room, hurry down the hall and knock on his door.

When he answers, I have to take a breath.

My God, how did he get more handsome? And how did I not notice that he has a dimple in his right cheek?

"Ho Ho Ho?"

Chapter Four

Dylan

Maddie frowns and then looks down at her adorable pajamas and laughs.

"This was our present this morning," she says and shrugs her shoulder. "We all got pajamas. Even the grandparents."

"Your *grandparents* are here?" I ask in surprise, taking her hand to bring her into my room.

"Three sets of them," she says. "I told you, it's a big family. What about yours?"

"My what?"

She sits in the chair and crosses her legs. I want to yank her to me and see exactly what she has on under those PJs.

"Your family, Dylan."

"Right. Sorry, you distract me."

Her eyes widen, and then she looks down at herself again. "You can't see anything."

"Exactly. My imagination is running wild. Anyway, I have both of my parents, and they're still married. A few aunts and uncles, cousins sprinkled around here and there."

"Any siblings?" She flips her dark hair over her shoulder.

"I had a younger brother, but he passed of childhood cancer when he was three."

Her jaw drops, and then her face turns sad, the way I'm used to when I tell people about my brother.

"I'm sorry, Dylan."

"You didn't kill him. The cancer did. And it was a really long time ago. I'm mostly just close to my parents."

"The Montgomery family adopted me when I was small." She frowns as if she didn't mean to tell me that, but I nod, wanting to hear more. "I don't remember much about my biological father, which is weird because we lived with him until I was at least in kindergarten. He wasn't exactly the salt of the Earth. Got in with the wrong people, and they killed him. I still don't know the full story. But my mom moved us to Seattle, where her cousin lived. They were close. And the cousin, Stacy, is married to Isaac Montgomery, the eldest sibling. Mom met Caleb, who made it his life's mission to protect us, and then they fell in love."

"I think that's probably the CliffsNotes version of the story."

"Of course, but I was a kid. I don't remember a lot of it. I *do* remember that Dad—Caleb—made us feel so safe. And he was kind of moody at first. Of course, he's always a little moody."

She grins, and I can see that she loves her parents a lot.

"They had Drew, and that rounded out the family. Basically, Josie and I went from just having our mom to having the biggest family ever."

"And you love it."

"Yeah." She grins and nods slowly. "I do. They're loud and sometimes obnoxious, but they're also really cool. Uncle Luke gave a nice little speech this morning and said that he brought us all here because we've all grown up, and the family is changing. He thought it would be nice to enjoy this time together."

"And here I am, taking you away from them."

And yet, I don't feel guilty at all.

"Well, they're watching *It's a Wonderful Life* in a conference room. Knowing Uncle Luke, it probably looks like a movie theater in there now. They won't miss me—not for a while, anyway. Did you get some work done?"

"I did. I also talked with my mom to wish her a merry Christmas, and I finally got some sleep."

"You've been busy."

I grin at her, watching as her pupils dilate. The attraction here is definitely *not* one-sided, and that eases my mind.

She's here because she wants to be. Maybe she feels the pull as strongly as I do.

"So, what are we doing?" Maddie's cheeks darken. "I mean...what is this, exactly?"

"What do you want it to be?"

She sighs, rubbing her hands over her face.

"Hey, I'm not here to stress you out, Maddie. If you don't want to be here or see me anymore, you can tell me to fuck off and I will. No harm, no foul."

She shakes her head and then laughs. "No, that's not what I meant. I'm pretty bad at this whole boy-girl thing."

"Trust me when I say you are absolutely *not* bad at this. What do you need from me, honey? Do you need to set some boundaries?"

"Maybe. I don't know." She looks nervous, and that's something I won't have. So, I cross to her, lift her out of the chair, and then sit and settle her in my lap. "Wow, you're strong."

"I can write *and* go to the gym." I kiss her chin. "Let's talk this out so I can get you naked after."

She giggles and then shakes her head. "This is way out of my realm of experience. I'm not exactly spontaneous or adventurous by any stretch of the imagination. My family never fails to remind me how boring I am."

"Then they don't know you well. Because I don't find you boring at all."

She bites her lip, and I reach up and tug it out from between her teeth with my thumb.

"I'll be doing the biting around here, sweetheart. As soon as we settle this."

"You know, you're really good at the flirting."

"Is that what I'm doing?"

"Aren't you?"

"Sure, a little. But I'm also just saying what's on my mind. I want you, period."

"So, you want sex."

"Absofuckinglutely." I kiss her chin again. "But I like this, too. Talking and hanging out. We can do both."

"And then, at the end of the week, we go home."

I tilt my head to the side, watching her. "If that's what you want."

"A vacation fling."

That doesn't sit well in my stomach, but I nod at her. "As I said, if that's what you want, you got it."

"Okay." She nods as if she's just made an important decision, and then she wraps her arms around my neck and kisses me like she's starving.

We don't make a move to take it further. I'm happy sitting here and kissing the hell out of her. Feeling her melt against me as I explore her mouth thoroughly. I didn't get to do this earlier when anyone could have walked in on us at any given moment.

So, I'm happy to take my time now.

I nibble that lower lip and grin when she moans.

When I make my way over her jawline and down to her neck, she sighs.

And when my hand slides up her side to cup her breast over the cotton of her pajamas, she gasps.

"The noises you make should come with a warning label," I inform her and begin unbuttoning her top.

"What would it say?" She's breathless, and her eyes are heavy-lidded with lust.

"*Warning: May Cause a Hard-on.*"

She giggles, but when I push against her hip, she bites that lip again and watches me with bright brown eyes.

"We might want to move out of the chair," she suggests.

"Oh, I'll have you in the chair," I promise as I stand with her in my arms. "Later. But first, I need to do this the way I wanted to on that damn plane."

"To be fair, we were hampered by space."

I laugh and lay her on the mattress. "We aren't now. By the way, I found some condoms."

"Hallelujah."

I quickly strip out of my shirt, then shuck off my jeans. Her gaze hungrily moves over my body.

It stops at my cock.

Without a word, she sits up and wraps her hand around me. Before I can say a word, her sweet mouth is around the tip, and I'm catapulted into the fucking stratosphere.

"Oh, hell yes."

She moans and works me over with that hot mouth.

"Look at me."

She immediately complies, and those brown pools gazing up at me as she sucks me deep is almost my undoing.

But I don't want to come like this. Not this time.

So, I urge her back onto the bed and laugh when she scowls at me.

"I wasn't done."

"You have to be for now, because I don't want to come in that perfect little mouth of yours. And I need to look at you."

"I'm not really one to worry about these things," she says as I go back to unbuttoning her top once more, "but I'm not exactly *perfect*. Like, I have cousins with fit bodies because that's what they do all the time, but I work at a desk and I don't go to the gym like I should and—"

I push up and cover her mouth with mine, effectively shutting her up.

"Guess what, baby?"

"What?"

"I'm so fucking attracted to you that I can't think about anything else. I want you to the point of feeling like a goddamn animal. It's primal. It's instinctual. I don't give a fuck about anything you might be worried about. I *like* curves. I need something to hold onto. So, don't worry about not being what you think is *perfect* because you're pretty fucking spectacular to me."

Her mouth opens, closes, then opens again.

"Well, okay, then."

"Okay."

When I have her top unbuttoned all the way, I spread it apart and discover that there's no bra underneath.

"You were going to watch movies with no bra?"

She laughs and then sighs when I plant a kiss right between her excellent breasts.

"It's baggy, and a dark movie. A girl should be comfy."

"Damn right." Fuck me, her tits are amazing. Round with nipples the color of her lips, begging for my mouth to be on them.

I wrap my lips around one and tug, grazing my teeth lightly over the areola. Maddie squirms under me.

"Holy shit, Dylan, hurry up."

"Buckle up, sweetheart. I'm just getting started."

"You're going to kill me."

I laugh and slide my hand under the waistband of her pants, lifting my head in surprise when I find she's commando.

She's slick and warm as my fingers slide into her, and she arches her back and bites her lip.

"Jesus Christ," I mutter before pulling her pants down her hips and tossing them over my shoulder. She's spread out before me like a goddamn holiday feast.

And I don't see even one flaw in this gorgeous woman.

"How badly do you want to watch those movies?" I ask her.

"Huh? What movies?"

I grin and kiss my way up her thigh. "Holiday movies, babe."

"Oh. Right. Um." She gasps when I lick the tender flesh where her leg meets her center. "Don't really care about them right now."

"Good. Because I plan to be here for a while. You'll probably miss the movie."

I brush my nose against her clit, then tickle it with the tip of my tongue. Every muscle in my body is on high alert.

My cock is screaming for her.

But it'll have to wait because I plan to drive her fucking wild before I'm inside of her.

"Tell me what your favorite flower is."

When I suck one lip into my mouth, she grabs onto my hair and pulls, making it hurt so damn good.

"Tell me, Maddie."

"Why?"

"Because it's fun to distract you. Tell me what your favorite flower is."

"Sunflower." She swallows hard, and I lick her again.

"Tell me about—"

"No way." She sits up, pushes on my shoulders, and I let her urge me onto my back. She kisses my collarbone as she straddles my lap. "No more talking, Dylan. You're driving me mad."

"Good." But I grip her hips as she rises to let me inside her. "Wait. Hold on."

I roll over with Maddie still on top of me and reach for a condom.

"Oops." She laughs and takes it from me. "We can't forget this part."

"No. We can't."

I move to open the packet, but she plucks it from my fingers. "I've got this."

Chapter Five

Maddie

Dylan's eyes narrow as he leans back on his elbows. I'm not shy at all when I tear the packet with my teeth. And then, with my eyes locked on his, I roll the condom down his length.

He hisses in a breath.

I grin in satisfaction.

"You like that, don't you?" he asks.

"What's that?"

"Making me want to lose my shit."

I laugh and lean down to kiss him. "Of course, I do. I believe that's my main goal this week."

"Yeah, well, you're good at it." He cups my face, brushing his thumb over the apple of my cheek as he takes my mouth, nibbling and licking. I sink over him.

I have to rest my forehead on his as I seat myself fully on him and *breathe.*

"Goddamn, it's like you were made for me," he whispers, and a thrill runs through me. It *does* feel that way when we're together like this.

So, of course, the universe would throw him at me, barely long enough to enjoy for a week.

Dylan falls back onto the bed, and I begin to move, just a gentle rocking motion, back and forth, grinding down on him until he grits his teeth, and his fingertips bite into the flesh of my hips.

I can't get enough of him. The pressure builds within me, and I can't stop the friction between us, the press of my clit against his pubis. Just when I'm about to come, he rears up to take my breast in his mouth and tugs *hard*.

I fling my head back and succumb to the mind-numbing pleasure that sweeps through me. My body vibrates with it, and I don't bother trying to cover the noises I make as I convulse around him.

Dylan growls, lifts me off him, and is suddenly behind me in one smooth move, my ass in the air. He pushes right back inside me in one masterful maneuver that leaves me speechless.

And then, he does something I've only read about in books.

He *smacks my ass*.

"Holy shit," I mutter and grip the covers as he pushes into me, roughly, over and over again, making me climb that mountain of pleasure once more.

"So fucking hot," he growls. "So goddamn amazing."

He's talking about *me*.

His incredible voice, coupled with the delicious things he's doing to my body, sends me into oblivion once more.

This time, his fingers clench the globes of my ass as he pushes one last time inside of me and then follows me over the edge.

"Did I hurt you?" His voice is rough, his breaths coming fast as he pulls out and turns me to face him, framing my face in his hands. "Shit. I'm sorry, Maddie."

"You didn't hurt me." My hands come around his wrists, and I can't look away from the fire in his gorgeous green eyes. "You did *not* hurt me."

"I was rough—"

I press a finger to his lips and grin. "I liked it. I didn't know that was a thing for me, but I liked it. You didn't hurt me."

He rests his forehead against mine and lets out a sigh of relief.

"So, you liked it, huh?"

"Yeah." I swallow hard, still catching my breath. "Who would have thought?"

He laughs and leaves the bed to clean up. I follow him into the bathroom, wrap myself in his robe, and boost onto the sink while he starts the shower.

"Wanna join me?" he asks, pointing to the stream of water that's already steaming up the room.

"Nah, I wanna watch."

"A voyeur."

"Apparently. I'm learning all kinds of things about myself on this trip."

Dylan braces his hands on either side of the vanity at my hips and drags his nose back and forth across mine. "Same goes."

I smile and kiss him softly.

"Spend the day with me tomorrow," he says.

My first reaction is to agree immediately, but then I remember that I'm actually here on a *family* vacation and should spend some time with them.

"I think I have to go play on a glacier with my family." I bite my lip. "You could come with us."

Shit. Why did I suggest that? He doesn't want to hang out with my *family*, and I'm not sure I want him to.

"You're not ready for that." He gently drags a finger down my cheek. "And that's okay. Go hang with your fam. We can have dinner together after. I have plenty of work to do anyway."

"That's what I should be doing." I sigh as he moves away from me. "Working."

"Is what your sister said true? That you don't take any time off?"

"I took a week off last year because I had to have my gall bladder removed. I put it off for as long as I could, but I was *so sick*. It had to go. Aside from that, I don't take much time off. And, yeah,"—I hold up my hand before he can say anything—"you can tell me that's not healthy and that I need to make time for *fun*, but I like to work."

"Taking a vacation here and there doesn't mean you don't like your job, Maddie. It's just basic maintenance. You need a break."

"That's what everyone says."

I look down and wish that just *one* person in my life understood me.

"Hey." He tips up my chin and kisses my forehead. "I get it. I like to work, too. Just don't forget to decompress a little sometimes. It's good for you."

"I think that's what I'm doing this week."

He nods. "Yeah, well, one week out of your entire life isn't enough."

"Why don't you stop judging me and get in the shower? Give me a little show."

He raises an eyebrow. "Changing the subject, are we?"

"Absolutely. Grab some soap, handsome."

* * * *

Splat.

Something cold and hard hits my back, and I spin to find my cousin, Keaton, laughing his ass off.

"Oh, yeah?" I scoop up some snow and hurl it at him, hitting him right in the chest. "Back at you, you little twerp."

"Snowball fight!" Drew yells. Suddenly, I'm in the middle of a snow war on a glacier in Iceland, having the time of my damn life.

There's laughter and yelps from icy snow ending up down shirts, and when we're finished, we're all spread out on the ground, laughing and trying to catch our breath.

"You're pretty fast for an old lady." My teenage cousin Finn smirks at me.

"Do you want me to kill you right here and now?"

He laughs and lays back on the snow. "Right."

"My dad was a SEAL. Do you think he didn't teach me how to kill people and make it look like an accident?"

Finn just laughs and then halfheartedly tosses a little snow my way. "You love me. You wouldn't kill me."

"Maim, then."

"Nah. I'm too cute."

"You used to be." I tilt my head to the side, watching him. His blue eyes are bright with laughter. "Now, you're just a weird little teenager."

"That's my job." He shrugs a shoulder, completely unconcerned with my comment. "Come on, I'll help you up."

He stands and offers me a hand, which I take. But instead of standing, I pull him onto the snow next to me, and it sends us into another fit of giggles.

"Well, look at this." I gaze up into my sister's smiling face. "My one and only sister, having *fun*."

"Oh, don't start."

Finn stands once more, holding out his hand for mine. This time I grab it and climb to my feet.

"And that, my gorgeous friends, is how a family has a snowball fight in Iceland!" Sophie is talking to her phone, per usual, panning the camera around at all of us. She's an incredible fitness influencer with millions of followers. I think people love her because she's *real*. Fun. And she likes to incorporate the family into her videos, bringing in guests like Uncle Will and Haley—who's a runner. She even hung out with Drew and his team for a day.

Heck, even *I* follow Sophie, and I don't run unless something's chasing me.

"I like that you're enjoying yourself," Josie adds and kisses my numb cheek. "It's fucking cold out here."

"It feels good, though," Olivia says as she and Stella join us. The guys are off somewhere, exploring.

I like that my cousin's men are friends.

"I *love* your coat." I run my hand down the sleeve of Liv's coat and sigh. "Where did you get it?"

"I made it." She gives me a toothy grin. "I can make you one if you want."

"I won't need a coat that heavy for Seattle, but it's seriously beautiful."

I pet her one more time and then sigh.

I really am having fun.

But I kind of miss Dylan.

Which is so weird.

"Are you mooning over your man?" Josie asks, and I feel my eyes widen. "What? They can know," she adds.

"We *already* know," Stella says and bumps me with her shoulder. "Josie told us."

"You said you *wouldn't* tell."

"Come on, it's juicy news. And I only told the cousins, not the parents."

"Gee, I guess that makes it all better then."

"Come on, you know we live for this stuff." Olivia pats my shoulder and grins. "You should have brought him today so we could all check him out."

"No way. It's just a vacation fling. He doesn't need to meet the family."

"Well, the alternative is splitting your time between him and us while you're here, and that's not fun," Stella points out. "So, I think you should just spend time with him."

"I agree," Josie pipes up.

"This is a *family* holiday vacation," I remind them. "That I didn't pay for. It would be rude and just plain wrong for me to ignore everybody for the rest of the trip."

"I didn't suggest that," Stella points out. "Hey, Luke said we can do as much or as little as we want. I say you spend most of your time with Dylan. You can still hang with the fam for dinner or whatever. But you can see all of us whenever you want back home."

"Not in Iceland, though."

"Are you always this stubborn?" Liv asks, propping her hands on her hips.

"Yeah," Josie says with a nod. "She is. I agree, Mad. Go have all the wild sex in the world. Fuck him until he's *blind*."

"You're such a lady."

Josie snorts. "Then, all of us cousins can meet up, and you can tell us all about it."

"I *knew* there were ulterior motives."

"Seriously, I don't remember the last time I saw you this happy." Liv smiles at me. "So, go. Be happy. I hear he's a dish. I want to meet him."

"You know, we're planning a cousins' night the last night we're at the lagoon. Bring him. The parents won't be there, so there's no pressure for him to make a good impression. It'll be casual and fun, and we can check him out." Stella grins. "It's perfect."

"If he wants to come, I'll bring him. I like him, guys. It's been a *good* time so far, and we're only a few days in."

"As of tomorrow, we're halfway into the trip," Josie reminds me. "So, you'd better stick closer to him and enjoy every minute."

"Wow. Time flies when you're having good sex." I smile at them and then do a little shimmy on the snow, careful not to slip and fall on my ass. "And, let me just say, it's *really* good sex."

"Attagirl," Stella says, holding up her hand for a high-five. "We will have drinks soon, and you can tell us *everything*."

"All the things," Liv agrees. "I think I see the guys making their way back. I wonder if they found the abominable snowman."

"Probably just a head cold," Stella says as we watch the guys walking our way. "It's hella cold out here. Why didn't we go somewhere tropical for Christmas? Who comes to freaking *Iceland* for the holidays? It says right in the name that it's fucking cold."

"Come on. It's cold, but it's pretty." I glance around at the gorgeous mountains. "Also, I wouldn't have met Dylan somewhere tropical."

"True." Stella grins when Gray blows her a kiss. "Let's go back to the hotel so I can have some good sex, too."

"Good idea," Liv says, eyeing Vaughn.

"Brax won't complain about that at all," Josie adds, and I think of Dylan and the smile I know will be waiting for me when I knock on his door.

"Let's go."

Chapter Six

Dylan

"I can't eat shark."

Maddie stares at the food on my fork in absolute horror.

"Why? It's fish."

"It's not fish. It's *shark*."

"I hate to break it to you, but it's a traditional food here, and it's really just fish."

I eat the bite and swallow as she stares on in concern. "See? Fish."

I decided tonight was a good night to take Maddie into Reykjavík for the evening to tour the city and make our way through the restaurants.

A food walk of sorts.

We started with cocktails and appetizers and are now having our entrées at one of my favorite places in the city.

"I'd like to try the fish stew," she says, shaking her head and peering down at the menu.

"Are you a picky eater?"

"I never thought so." She takes a sip of water as if she has to get rid of the taste of shark, even though she hasn't had any.

God, she's fucking adorable.

"You must eat all kinds of food since you travel so much."

"Yeah, there's not much I *haven't* tried. If shark makes you queasy, you probably don't want to go to places in Asia where they eat bugs and stuff."

Her skin goes a little green at the thought, and I laugh.

"I think you're safe with the stew. And we'll get some bread. After this, we have to walk down the street to get a traditional Icelandic hotdog."

Maddie blinks in surprise. "A hotdog? I thought that was an American thing."

"I don't know the history of the hotdog," I admit thoughtfully and take another bite of the shark. "But I can tell you that they're famous here."

"Nice, I like a hotdog now and then. Wait." Her face sobers. "Is it made out of shark and lamb head?"

The server interrupts us, and Maddie requests stew and bread. When we're alone once more, I smile at her.

"First of all, the hotdog stand is *tiny*—like something you'd see on the street in New York. It's been there for more than eighty years, and it's never missed a day of being open, no matter the weather."

"Wow." She looks impressed, so I keep going.

"Second, I do know that while American hotdogs are made of pork or beef—sometimes chicken—Icelandic hotdogs are made from lamb meat. But not the head. And no shark. It looks like a regular hotdog, Maddie."

"Okay." She sits back as the server sets a steaming bowl of soup with crusty bread and butter before her. "Wow, this looks good."

"Yeah, it does."

She tries a bite and then looks up at me in surprise. "It *is* good."

"Told you."

She digs in, and I enjoy watching her eat. She's not shy about it, and it's refreshing.

"How's the bread?"

She takes a bite and then sighs the way she does when I'm buried deep inside her, and she's about to come.

It makes me squirm in my seat.

"Damn, I think they made this fresh. Today."

"It's likely."

I grin, glad she's enjoying her meal. We take our time with it, and when we're ready to leave, Maddie takes my hand and leans her head on my shoulder as we walk out into the brisk evening air.

"This is fun," she says. "I've never done anything like this before."

"I like to do it in every new city. It's a great way to learn what the locals eat. That's usually a better bet than eating at the tourist spots."

"Although I suspect this hotdog stand *is* a tourist spot."

"One of the rare, amazing ones," I agree as we walk down the sidewalk, hand in hand, the twinkling lights of the season sparkling above us. The snow and ice crunch under our winter boots, and we can see our breath in the air.

It's invigorating and romantic.

"Is that it?" Maddie asks, pointing to the small line about a city block ahead.

"That's it. It doesn't look like we'll have to wait long."

The line is even shorter when we get there.

"I think we should share one," Maddie suggests. "This is a *lot* of food."

"We'll share one, then."

I place our order, and when the dog comes out, it smells like heaven.

"You take the first bite."

I hold it out to her, and she nibbles off the end of the hotdog.

"Wow," she says, chewing. "That's good."

We keep walking as we eat, taking in the sights and pointing things out.

"I might have to come back to town when this shop is open," she says, peering in a window. "My mom's birthday is coming up. She'd love that bracelet."

"Then we'll come back for it tomorrow."

She glances up at me, her nose a little red from the cold, and grins. "You don't have to come back with me."

"I want to." I kiss her red-gloved hand. "I'm going to spend as much time with you as humanly possible. You having your own room is a complete waste of money at this point."

She snorts and then continues down the sidewalk.

"I haven't seen any northern lights since I've been here." She's looking up and would have tripped on the broken sidewalk if I didn't physically move her out of the way. "I thought they'd be going all the time." She glances at me.

"It's not as simple as flipping a switch," I remind her, and she looks up again, wrinkling her nose. "They usually come out to dance later in the evening. You'll see them. I promise."

Something in my tone must prompt her to look at me once more, but I only smile.

Oh, yeah, she's going to see them.

"I think it's time for dessert."

She laughs. "Is that a euphemism?"

"No. Although that will come later. Literally."

"Ha-ha, funny guy."

"We have to get actual dessert. I personally think you need to try the homemade ice cream here because there's absolutely nothing like it anywhere. But they also make some incredible cakes that you might like."

"I'm stuffed. I basically had *two* dinners."

"We'll share something, then. Come on."

I lead her into another of my favorite restaurants and request a dessert menu when we're seated.

But rather than order just one thing, I ask for a little of everything, and the plate is heaping when it arrives.

"*Dylan*," Maddie breathes. "We can't eat all of this."

"But we can try it all." I wink at her and take a bite of almond cake. "Go on, have some."

She has a bite of ice cream and moans, making me regret our prolonged excursion.

I want her in bed *now*.

"Man, that's good. You can just roll me back to the hotel."

"No problem."

* * * *

"Okay, that was fun."

We've just returned to the hotel and are walking through the lobby, hand in hand, full from an evening of food.

"I'm glad you liked it."

"Liked it? I might have gained ten pounds, but it was worth it."

I see a man walk out of the elevator. He's tall, built, and looks dangerous, even with the gray streaking his hair.

When Maddie sees him, she stiffens and drops my hand.

"Shit, that's my *father*. Go away."

She pushes me aside and then rushes ahead of me, trying to act like she doesn't know me.

It's fucking hilarious.

I stay back and lean against a column in the lobby, watching as the intimidating man's hard expression melts into mush when he sees his daughter.

He tugs Maddie in for a hug and asks her a question. Maddie nods, and his face softens even more before he pats her shoulder and then steps away.

She says something to him, and he returns to the elevator.

When the doors slide closed behind him, Maddie blows out a breath and hurries back over to me.

"I'm sorry," she says with a wince. "I'm *really* sorry."

"I guess it's not time for me to meet your father."

She frowns and walks beside me, but she doesn't retake my hand. "This is just a vacation fling. No meeting the parents."

Right. A *vacation fling*, as she continues to put it. But the more I'm with her, the more I realize that I don't want to settle for just one week with this woman. I want to see more of her when we get home.

I may want to have her in my life for a long, long time.

But, at the end of the day, it doesn't really matter what I want. It's up to Maddie. If she only wants a short thing while we're here, then that's what I'll have to settle for, no matter how much it irritates the shit out of me.

"You got quiet," she says in the elevator on our way up to my room. "I really *am* sorry that I shoved you like that. I panicked."

"It was actually amusing." I kiss her temple. When the elevator stops on our floor, I lead her down to my door. "I have plans for tonight."

"No more food," is her immediate, almost panicked response. "I can't do it, Dylan. I'll explode."

"No." I shut the door behind us and then kiss the tip of her nose. "No food. Not for a while anyway. But I do have something to show you."

"Really? I've seen it, but I'm always happy to see it again."

"You're funny."

That makes her snort. "Right. Funny-looking, maybe."

Now *that* makes me pause. I push her against the wall and lean into her.

"That's *not* funny, Maddie."

"It's just an expression."

"I don't like it." I nibble those delicious lips that still taste like ice cream. "I don't like it at all. You're fucking gorgeous."

"I mean, I love that you think so. But, realistically, I'm just a girl, Dylan."

My girl, I think.

But I don't say it.

"You're a beautiful woman," I insist and nibble my way down her jawline to her slim neck. "And if I have to work my ass off for the few days we have left here to make you believe it, well, that's exactly what I'll do."

"You're sweet."

I pull back and look her in the eyes. "No. I'm not being sweet. I'm being honest. Do you think I take the time to seduce just any woman I meet while on a business trip?"

"I don't know." She swallows hard. "I don't mean that to be hurtful or rude. I really *don't* know."

"Well, I don't. I told you before, it was different the minute I saw you. And I don't know why. I just know what I felt. And I thank any of the gods who might be listening for dropping you into my life because, man, have you made it more fun."

A slow smile spreads across her gorgeous face. "That might be the nicest thing anyone has ever said to me."

"It's true." God, I can't get enough of her. I can't stop looking at her, running my hands over her, wanting to feel her close to me. "I'm so completely taken with you, I can't think about much of anything else. You're beautiful and funny and just a hell of a great girl to be with."

"Wow."

"I hate that anyone in your life ever made you feel otherwise. Even your family."

"No one has tried to make me feel bad." It's a whisper, said as she stares at my lips. "I think they worry about me more than anything."

"Maddie."

She raises her gaze to mine. "Yes, Dylan?"

"Remember when I told you that I had something to show you?"

"I think so."

I grin. "I still do, honey."

"Okay."

Chapter Seven

Maddie

"Holy shit, Dylan."

He has my hand grasped in his tightly as he leads me up a short set of steps, through a door, and out onto the hotel's roof.

All I can do is stare in wonder at the little lantern next to a futon covered in blankets that rests in the middle of the roof.

"Did the resort do this?" I ask as he leads me to it.

"I asked them to," he replies with a grin and holds the blankets up for me to climb under.

"They're electric." I blink up at him in surprise. "Nice."

"It's fucking cold out here." He laughs as he joins me, bringing me close to his side before reaching over and turning off the lantern. "The darker it is, the better to see the show."

We both look up into a clear winter sky. The stars are *ridiculous*. "I've never seen stars like this." My voice is a whisper.

"There's hardly any light noise here," he replies softly. "You can see everything. The stars, comets if they're around, the Milky Way. And…look."

He points to the horizon, which is just starting to turn green.

"They'll build." His voice is a promise as he takes my hand in his and kisses my knuckles before linking our fingers together. "We just have to give it some time."

"This is…*romantic*."

"You sound surprised."

He kisses the top of my head, and I feel it all the way to my toes. It's always the same whenever he touches me. This sense of awareness washes over and through me, and it's the warmest, safest feeling I've ever experienced.

"I guess I'm surprised," I admit. "I didn't think romance was usually part of a vacation fling."

He sighs, and the next thing I know, he's turned and framed my face in his hands.

"Let's drop the label from now on, okay? There are no rules or expectations here. We're enjoying each other, and I knew when we arrived that I wanted to lie under the aurora borealis with you. I don't give a shit that we're only here for a few more days."

"I didn't mean to make you mad."

"I'm not." He swallows and drags his thumb across my cheek. "I just don't like the label."

"Then it's gone." I lean in to kiss his lips, drinking in the taste of him. "Thanks for this. It's already beautiful."

"There's so much more to come."

He sits back, and I gasp when I look into the sky once more.

I can't help myself.

It looks like figures in green and blue dresses dancing through the heavens.

"Oh, my God."

"Magical, aren't they?"

"I've never seen anything like it."

"I know." He clears his throat. When I glance his way, I see that he's staring at *me*, not the sky. "I've never seen anything like you."

I don't try to brush away the compliment or even shyly lower my gaze because I can see that he means every word.

He's not just trying to get in my pants.

I mean, we've already been there and done that.

"I've never *met* anyone like you," I admit softly. Dylan is someone I could fall in love with if I don't watch myself. "I'm having a really great week."

"Excellent." He's warm next to me, and when I move to straddle him, he doesn't stop me.

"I need my mouth on you." I kiss him, lightly at first, just grazing my lips back and forth. Then, I do the same with my nose over his. His hands tighten on my ass, but he doesn't urge me to move faster.

He's patient.

"I love that you're so thoughtful." I kiss his cheek. "And kind." I kiss his ear. "You're incredibly sexy, and your muscles just go on for days."

"And here I was going for weeks."

I chuckle and lick my way down his neck. He sucks in a breath, and his hands push up under my shirt and over my ribs.

"I've wanted to make love to you like this all week," he admits.

"And here we are, with hundreds of people below us in the hotel, under the stars and northern lights, getting naughty."

"*Naughty.*" He says it with a grin. "Oh, I like that."

"I thought you might."

He takes control of the kiss and urges me onto my back on the futon. His mouth is more urgent, his hands a little greedy as they move over me, sending me into a lusty frenzy.

"Open your eyes," he commands. When I do, the lights above almost cast a halo around him.

"Wow."

"I can see them in your eyes," he whispers, pulling my pants down my legs. We're burrowed under the covers, getting naked outside, and I don't even care.

Who am I?

We move fervently now, removing the necessary clothing, and Dylan plucks a condom out of his back jeans pocket before casting the pants aside.

"Always a planner," I say.

"Hell, yes. I want to fuck you every chance I get."

God, he makes me feel so beautiful. So desirable.

I don't ever want this week to end.

Dylan protects us both, pushes inside me, and with our gazes locked, proceeds to make love to me under the most spectacular display in the sky I've ever seen. It's sexy and moving, and when we both climax, we cling to each other.

When his lips tenderly brush mine, and he moves a piece of hair from my cheek, I know without a doubt that this week has changed me.

I've fallen in love with him.

I just couldn't help it.

"Are you okay?" he asks.

"Oh, yeah. You?"

He sighs, still watching me, something in those green eyes that I can't put a label on.

"I'm fantastic."

He kisses me again, and then we right ourselves, pull on our clothes, and huddle fully under the blankets to watch the sky.

"I might fall asleep out here," I admit.

"I don't think anyone will mind."

* * * *

"I love brunch," Sophie announces the next morning. The whole family has gathered in Luke and Nat's suite for a spread fit for kings and queens.

"How do you eat croissants and still look like that?" Erin asks her. "Is that on your program?"

"Honey, it's all about moderation. Also, did you know that in Europe—and most other places in the world—bread isn't bad for you? Don't even get me started on what goes into our food in the US."

"Please, don't get her started," Sophie's brother, Liam, says while rolling his eyes. "She won't shut up, and we're supposed to be enjoying this."

I toss a blueberry at Liam. "Hey. Be nice to her. She's badass."

"Didn't say any differently," Liam says, picking the blueberry off his shirt to eat it.

"I like what Iceland has done for you," my aunt Meredith says thoughtfully, eating a strawberry. "You're quick to smile and not so quiet."

"It's almost as though we have our *old* Maddie back," Aunt Alecia agrees. She's weaving her daughter Emma's long dark hair into Viking braids, watching a YouTube tutorial as she goes. "I remember when you were a kiddo. You were so outgoing. So gregarious."

"Sometimes, annoying," Drew says, and I flip him the bird. "See? Still annoying."

"And then something happened when you were about...oh, I don't know, in middle school or so," my dad adds, and I look around, realizing the room has gone quiet, and everyone is listening.

Now, I'm uncomfortable.

"*Did* something happen, baby girl?" Grandpa Steven asks.

I shrug a shoulder and reach for my bowl of fruit. "Who can remember back that far?"

"Hey." Uncle Matt takes my hand and smiles down at me. I don't know what it is about his eyes, but they make a woman want to tell the truth, the whole truth, and nothing but the truth.

Maybe it's because he's a cop.

"You can tell us. I think we're all genuinely curious."

"I mean, am I that horrible to be around?"

"Not at all," Meg rushes to assure me. "You're one of my favorite people. But there was *definitely* a shift at that time."

I take in a deep breath and let it out slowly. "It's not like I was hurt or anything. I just remember some kids in my class were little jerks in the sixth grade."

"Most kids are," Jules says, making me smile.

"Hey," Finn, the youngest at sixteen, says with a scowl. "I'm not a little jerk."

"Oh, you have your moments, my darling son," Aunt Nic says with a laugh.

"Anyway," I continue, "they just weren't nice. Looking back, I guess they were kind of bullies. I know that I could be loud and probably too outgoing sometimes. They often told me to shut it. Said I was too much. Needed to tone it down because no one wanted to be around me."

My dad's eyes narrow, and I shake my head.

"It's fine. I discovered that you can take in more when you're quiet. Listen more. And I really did like studying. I guess my priorities changed."

"Basically, some little fuckwits decided to be assholes and bully you, so you shut up and took it." This comes from Drew, who looks like he wants to punch someone. "Oh, hell no."

"It was a long, *long* time ago. I like my life, you guys. I'm totally *fine*."

"You may be fine," Mom says and walks around the table to wrap her arm around my shoulders. "And you're a wonderful woman, but the next time someone tells you you're too much, you tell them to go find *less.*"

"I'll tell my sixth-grade self that."

"Good." She kisses my cheek. "Now, back to the original point. I am *so* glad you're enjoying your vacation. You practically glow."

"Probably all the sex," Jules says, and I can feel my eyes practically bug out of my head.

"*Jules!*"

She looks around the room and then back at me. "What? It's not like we don't know. You're *glowing.* And good for you."

I hang my head in my hands and wish with all my might that the volcano we're sitting by would go ahead and erupt, ending my suffering.

"Don't worry," my Aunt Stacy says. "We'll have a girls' night and get all the details."

"I've never been more mortified in my life."

"Then you're doing really well," Natalie replies. "Like, *really* well."

* * * *

"My aunt announced to the whole family this morning that I look so happy because of all of the sex I've been having."

Dylan is driving us through the countryside to destinations unknown.

Well, unknown to *me.*

He knows where he's taking me.

"It's nice of them to notice my hard work," he says, making me laugh.

"The parents weren't supposed to know," I remind him. "And she said it in front of everyone, so I was mortified."

"You're in your thirties, Maddie. Do they think you're a nun?"

I watch the snow-covered hills as we pass and shake my head. "No, I'm sure not. It's just…uncomfortable."

"I'm sure you're the only one who feels that way. Here we go."

He parks and cuts the engine.

"We have to walk a bit, but I have crampons for our shoes."

"It's a good thing I brought the snow gear. You didn't tell me where we were going."

"It's a surprise."

He seems unconcerned as we get out of the car, and he helps me fasten the little things that wrap around my shoes, making them perfect for walking in snow and ice.

And then we set off down a path that's clearly been traveled quite a bit, although we seem to be the only ones here today.

As we walk farther from the road, I hear rushing water. And then, I see it.

"Wow."

Chapter Eight

Dylan

"Be careful." I step ahead of Maddie on the trail so I can catch her if she falls. "The path isn't steep, but it's wet and icy. Even so, it's worth the walk down."

"This is *incredible*," she breathes and braces her hand on my shoulder. "It's magical."

"Makes you believe in the magic that lives in Iceland, doesn't it?"

"It really does. I heard there's a witch museum here. That could be fun."

"I'll add it to the list for tomorrow." I glance back at her with a grin. "Okay, watch your step."

At the bottom of the falls, we look up at the water cascading through a cloak of ice and snow.

"It's sixty meters tall," I inform her, feeling a bit like a tour guide and not minding at all. I'd spend the rest of my life being Maddie's tour guide. There are so many places I'd love to show her. "And the story goes that there is Viking treasure hidden behind the falls in the cave."

"Well, I see a path that leads back there. Let's go check it out."

"We'll have to come back in the summer for that," I reply and tug her back to me when she starts setting off for the falls. "It's closed in the winter because it's too dangerous."

"That sucks," she mutters. "I may never get back here. You know how often I take vacations."

If I had my way, I'd change that immediately. Maddie is missing out on some amazing things in the world, and I want to show her all of them. Explore new ones with her.

But I'd better not mention any of it because…this is just a *holiday fling.*

"It's amazing that the water still falls, even through the ice and snow."

I follow her gaze up and breathe in the cold air. "It's fed by a glacier. Iceland is actually known for its amazing waterfalls."

"For being so small," she says in wonder, not taking her eyes off the cascade before us, "it's a really gorgeous country."

"I absolutely agree." To my surprise, Maddie links her arms around my waist and just holds on, her cheek pressed to my chest as she watches the water.

It's…*sweet. She* is sweet.

I kiss the top of her head and breathe her in. When I saw the beautiful woman on my flight, I had no idea that we'd end up like this mere days later. But, here we are.

And there's nowhere else I'd rather be.

"This was totally worth the two-hour drive," she announces, smiling up at me. Her expression sobers. "What's wrong?"

"Nothing at all."

"You were frowning."

I shake my head. "I think my face is just frozen. That's the expression I'm stuck with for a while."

She relaxes and then laughs. "It's freaking *cold* out here. Let's go warm up in the car."

Going up is a lot easier than the trek down, and it doesn't take us long to reach the vehicle.

With the engine running, we get the heaters blasting and then sigh in relief as three vehicles carrying tourists pull in next to us.

"Good timing," Maddie says. "We had the whole place to ourselves. What next?"

"Are you too frozen, or do you want to check out some more waterfalls?"

"What's the other alternative?"

"We could drive back to the city and do that shopping you mentioned before."

"I think I like that option. I don't want to forget the piece for my mom, and I think I'd like to swim. My cousins lent me a couple of bathing suits."

"You didn't bring any with you?"

"I thought I was coming here for only twenty-four hours," she reminds me as I put the car in gear and head back in the direction of the city. "I had to borrow all kinds of things from my cousins. It's a good thing I'm similar in size to some of them."

"Did you borrow what you're wearing now?" I eye the green top with its scoop neck that gives me a peek of her spectacular breasts.

"Yeah, this is Liv's. Hey, speaking of swimming, since tomorrow is our last day here, all the cousins are having what we call *cousins' night* at the lagoon. There will be drinks, food, and swimming. You're welcome to join us. No pressure, of course. Really. It won't hurt my feelings if you don't want to go, it's just usually a good time. We get together all the time for the cousins' nights when we're home in Seattle, and—"

"Maddie."

"Yeah?"

I reach over and grab her hand, lifting it to my lips. "I'd love to go. Thanks for inviting me."

"You don't have to feel obligated."

"I don't."

"Really?"

"Really. Listen, I don't usually do much of anything that I don't want to do, so if I didn't want to spend time with your cousins, I'd tell you."

"Good. Also, I should warn you that my cousin Liam has a tendency to go streaking if he's been drinking too much."

"Sounds like a fun crowd."

"You have no idea."

* * * *

"You did *not* have to buy me that necklace," Maddie insists as I unlock the door of my room and usher her inside. "Or the scarf. I mean, you even bought me socks."

"Your feet looked cold."

"How do you know? They were in my shoes."

I grin at her and toss the bags onto the chair by the window.

"I'm psychic."

"Uh-huh. Right. Sure, you are." She's smiling when I nudge her against the wall and lean into her, dragging my nose across her cheek. "You spoiled me today."

"I wanted to. Also, I had an ulterior motive."

Her brown eyes shine at that. "Oh? What was that?"

"I'm going to get you naked." I drag my fingertip down her chest, over the outside of her shirt, and to the waistband of her pants. "And you're going to wear only that necklace while I fuck you senseless."

"I mean, it's the least I can do."

Chapter Nine

Maddie

"I could tell you everyone's names, but you'll never remember them all, and it usually takes spreadsheets and graphs."

We're walking down to the pool, hand in hand, and I'm nervous. Not because I'm ashamed of Dylan *or* my family, but because I've just never brought a date to anything before.

I never liked anyone enough to bring them around my family before Dylan.

And isn't it just my luck that I won't ever see him again after tomorrow?

"It's going to be fine," he assures me and kisses my hand. The man always has his hands or lips on me, and I have to admit, it doesn't suck.

Not at all.

We walk out to the pool area, and I can't help but smile when I see the family gathered at one end of the space, talking and laughing. A few are in the milky blue pool, floating at the edge so they can be a part of the conversation.

"This is my first cousins' night," Finn announces as we approach. "Because this is a pool for *everyone*, not just those consuming alcohol. You can't kick me out."

I smirk at him and pat his cheek. "Since when do you have *stubble*?"

Finn just smiles and jumps into the pool.

"We always restrict our cousins' nights to only those of age," I explain to Dylan. "But I'm glad the littler ones, and by *little* I mean high school age, are here."

"Wait." Dylan stops short and stares down at me with wide eyes, then back at our crowd. "*All* of those people are your cousins?"

"Yep." I nod happily. "Well, Olivia, the gorgeous brunette sitting on that man's lap? She's a cousin. The guy is her fiancé. And then Stella's in the pool with *her* new fiancé, Gray. They got engaged on Christmas Day."

I scan the crowd and find my sister. "And you met Josie. Next to her is her boyfriend, Brax. The others are blood relatives."

"You weren't kidding when you said there are a lot of you."

"Oh, this doesn't even include all the parents and grandparents who are here."

He stares down at me and then shakes his head. "Wow."

"Come on, you two," Sophie calls out, gesturing for us to join them. "Don't be shy."

"You know I'm not," I reply. "Dylan was just surprised by how many of us there are."

"We're a handful." Sophie smiles and offers her hand to Dylan. "I'm Sophie. Don't worry about remembering it. After Maddie and Josie, I'm the oldest."

"Nice to meet you, Sophie."

Soph's eyes narrow. "I see what you did there. Repeat the name and you're more likely to remember it."

Dylan just smiles, and Sophie leans in to me.

"You were right. *Hot.*"

She walks away with a wink.

"Maddie, come over here." That comes from Olivia, who has climbed off Vaughn's lap. "I want to meet Dylan."

Slowly, over the course of several minutes, the others gather around. We're surrounded by Montgomery cousins, each trying to get a look at my date.

"I'm Vaughn." Olivia's guy holds out his hand to Dylan.

"I recognize you," Dylan replies.

"Are you a fan?" Vaughn asks but doesn't smile. My cousin snagged the hottest movie star in the world.

"Eh, you do fine."

There's silence for a moment, and then everyone laughs, including Vaughn.

"I like him," Vaughn announces.

Soon, everyone scatters once more. We load up plates full of food from a small buffet spread and snag drinks before sitting at a table with Josie and Brax.

"They're overwhelming," Brax says with a shrug. "I've been around for a long time, and they're *still* a little overwhelming."

"But fun," Josie points out. "We're a lot of fun. It's kind of funny how other hotel guests have come out to swim but gave us a wide berth."

"I'm afraid Liam is about to strip down any minute," I reply, shaking my head. "That man is a little *too* confident in his skin."

"I don't think anyone is drinking enough to do something like that." Josie sips her drink. "Not yet, anyway."

"What time is our flight tomorrow?" I've been avoiding the question, but I have to ask because I have to be *on* the plane.

"Early," Josie says with a wince. "Like six or something. But it's a private plane, so the flight isn't too bad."

"Does your family always fly privately?" Dylan asks.

"No," I reply, shaking my head. "Well, some of the parents do. Uncle Luke usually does. But for the most part, we all fly commercial. I think it was just about the same price to fly the whole family privately as it would have been to book first class."

"Probably," Josie agrees. "Have you been working much, Mad?"

"No." And the guilt of it takes up residence in my stomach. "And trust me when I say I'm going to get an earful about it from my boss on Monday."

"Why?"

I turn at Dylan's question. "What do you mean?"

"He knows you're on a holiday vacation with your family. You shouldn't be expected to work at all."

"You're preaching to the choir," Josie mutters.

"I know it seems that simple." I can't even muster up any anger at Dylan's point. "You know the expression: You teach people how to treat you?"

"I've heard it," he replies.

"Well, I've basically taught my boss that I'm available twenty-four-seven and will put in all the extra hours he needs. It's my own fault, really."

"Then *un*teach him." Dylan looks almost frustrated as he sits forward in his chair. "And if he doesn't like that you're no longer at his beck and call, find a different job."

"The family has no less than a dozen businesses that could use you," Josie reminds me.

"I know, but I always felt like that was cheating in a way. That I had to find a job that had nothing at all to do with the family."

"That's kind of bullshit," Brax says, surprising me. "You have a skill that could help your family, and you know you'd make a good living *working* for it. Also, they wouldn't take advantage of you like your current boss."

Three sets of eyes stare at me, and I can't help but squirm under the scrutiny.

"I might have to think about it. Maybe it'll depend on the reception I get when I'm back in the office next week."

"Why are you guys being so serious over here?" Haley asks when she walks up. "We need to swim and dance and enjoy ourselves before we go back to the real world tomorrow. Come on."

"I'm up for a swim," I announce and stand, pulling my coverup over my head and tossing it aside. "Why don't any of the women in our family wear one-pieces?"

"We do. We just didn't bring them," Stella answers, still in the water. "Now, get in here. The water is *divine*."

I dive in and swim a whole lap, back and forth, before surfacing and opening my eyes.

Dylan watches me hungrily from the edge of the pool.

"You're right. The water is excellent."

"He looks like he wants to eat you alive," Stella whispers to me.

"Yeah." I sigh and watch as he hops into the water. "Isn't it hot?"

* * * *

"You know..." My voice is a whisper in the darkness. "We haven't slept at all."

It's past three in the morning. Dylan and I hung out with the family until close to midnight and then returned to his room to ring in the new year together. We made love—twice. Once in the shower and once in the chair by the window.

Then we climbed into bed and have been talking ever since.

"I'll have plenty of time to sleep later." He pulls me closer, and I wrap my leg around his hip.

"I'm so glad I had this time with you. It was unexpected and a lot of *fun*, which I haven't had much of in a long time."

"Promise me you'll make time for it more often. And tell your boss to go fuck himself."

I can't help but rest my forehead on his chest and laugh. "I'll see what I can do. Where will your next adventure take you? Somewhere exotic like Chile or Argentina, or the Maldives?"

"London," he says, surprising me. "We're doing a documentary on Windsor Castle. Not necessarily about the royal family but the castle itself. Should be interesting. I've been doing research for a long time, and now it's time to do it on-site."

"I've always wondered about London."

"Never been?"

I shake my head. "No, but maybe I'll see if a few of the cousins want to take a girls' trip and go sometime."

"You should." He drags his fingers down my cheek and looks like he wants to say more.

Instead, he leans in close to press his lips to mine.

When he rolls me onto my back, the lovemaking is slow and sweet this time, still full of heat but with none of the usual urgency or white-hot passion that usually comes with sex with Dylan.

It's almost sad as we move together.

As his hands roam over me, it's as if he's memorizing every line so he can recall this moment in his memory after we've said goodbye.

I want to tell him I don't want to say goodbye tomorrow. That I want to stay in touch and maybe even see him whenever he's in the US.

But we agreed from the beginning that this was a holiday fling, and that was it.

No strings attached.

Our sighs are muted in the quiet darkness of the room, and when we both surrender to climax, it feels like an ending.

And that makes me profoundly sad.

And incredibly grateful.

We lie quietly, neither of us sleeping as the minutes tick by. When five o'clock hits, I sigh.

"I should really go and pack up my things. We're leaving in an hour."

Without a word, Dylan climbs out of bed, and we get dressed. He walks to my room with me and watches with a sober expression as I fill my suitcase and a plastic laundry bag from the hotel since I have so many extra, borrowed clothes now.

When it's all ready to go, I turn to him.

"I don't want to hurt your feelings, but I kind of don't want you to go down with me. I'd rather say goodbye here. Privately."

Dylan frames my face in his hands and sighs. "I understand. You are a brilliant, funny, beautiful woman, Maddie Montgomery. I had the best week with you."

"I did, too." I will the tears away as I smile up at him. "Thank you for everything. Sincerely. Iceland wouldn't have been the same without you. Please, be safe on your travels. It's kind of a scary world out there."

"I'll be safe," he promises before pressing his lips to mine one last time. "You do the same, Maddie."

I nod, purse my lips, and then reach for my bags. "Take care, Dylan."

I just can't say goodbye. I can't bring myself to utter the word as I walk away and head down the hall to the elevator.

I don't have to wait. When the doors open, Sophie and Haley are inside with their bags.

"Good morning," Haley says with a yawn.

I don't reply as I step inside and turn around in time to see Dylan disappearing behind the closing doors.

* * * *

I've been home for three days, and it's time to return to work. I'm still jet-lagged and a little sad, so the idea of walking into the office and dealing with my boss isn't exciting to me.

But a girl has to pay her bills.

I have my briefcase in hand and have just walked into my closet-sized office when my boss, Jim, follows me inside and shuts the door.

By the look on his round face, I can see he's not happy.

"I'm fucking disappointed in you," he says.

"Hello, Jim. My Christmas was lovely, thank you. And yours?"

"Don't get cute with me. You had a job to do, and you didn't do it. Now, we're behind and might have to pay fines with the IRS for things that didn't get filed in time."

"I worked *my ass off* before I went on vacation," I remind him. His face registers shock, likely because I'm standing up for myself. "I had all my clients filed and done. The fact that other accountants also went on vacation, and you expected me to do *their* jobs is completely ridiculous."

"You don't like it?" He puffs out his chest, and I know right here and now that I'm *so done* with this place. "There's the door."

I take a calming breath. "You know, I've worked here for a long time. I always did what I was told, worked far more hours than I was paid for—"

"You're on salary!"

"And I never argue. I don't make waves. And for all of that loyalty to the firm, you're going to stand there and tell me to leave because I decided to take a real vacation for the first time in eight years? You know what? I'll be walking out that door you so helpfully pointed out to me."

Jim starts to sputter, clearly not expecting me to call his bluff.

"Now just hold on there."

"No. No, I won't. Life's too short to work this hard for little to no reward. I quit."

I gather the few things I have in my office, which isn't much—I never really settled into the space with my stuff. And then I walk out.

And for the first time in a *long* time, I feel powerful.

Badass.

And maybe a little scared.

When I get to my townhouse, I call Josie.

"'Lo?"

"Did you work last night?" I frown at the dark TV. "I didn't think you went back until tonight."

"Jet lag." She yawns in my ear. "What's up?"

"I just quit my job."

"What?" She's awake now, and I can imagine her sitting up in bed as I relay what went down in my office this morning. "I never liked that jerk."

"Well, I don't work for him anymore."

"Good. I'm really proud of you, Mad."

"Thanks. I'm sure I'll be proud after I'm done being terrified. I have a mortgage to pay, you know."

"You have money saved. You'll be okay for a little while. Now you can do what *you* want to do."

"I want to be an accountant. I like it, Josie."

"Well, you can be an accountant somewhere that appreciates you. It'll come together. How are you otherwise?"

I sigh and sit on the couch, propping my feet on the coffee table. "I'll be okay."

"Honey, if you're sad and miss the man, just *call him.*"

"I don't think I can. We agreed—"

"Yeah, yeah. You agreed on vacation sex and nothing more. But, sometimes, we change our minds, Maddie. Call him. The worst he can say is no."

"I'll think about it."

"Okay. I need coffee. I'll come over later and we'll celebrate with mimosas and donuts."

"I won't pass that up."

Chapter Ten

Dylan

It's been a week since I last saw Maddie. I fucking miss her. I shouldn't have let her walk away without insisting we stay in touch.

Without saying *something*.

Because I've been damn miserable since I got back to Seattle.

"You're so moody," Mom says as she pours me a cup of coffee. "Did you have a bad time in Iceland?"

"No, I had a great time." I push my hands through my hair and sigh. "I met someone."

She pauses mid-pour and stares at me. "*What?*"

"Don't get too excited." I explain about Maddie, leaving out the sex parts because no man wants to tell his mom about that. By the time I'm done, the woman is beaming and probably hearing wedding bells in her head.

"Call her immediately."

I sip my coffee and shake my head. "I don't think so."

"You've been so grouchy since you got back. You're obviously miserable and in love with this woman."

"In love with her?" I scoff, but my stomach flutters. "I barely know her."

Mom just rolls her eyes. "You said she lives here in Seattle?"

"Yeah."

"Then call her. Or go see her."

"I've driven past her house." I wince, not meaning to admit that out loud. "I'm *not* a stalker, damn it."

"Of course, you're not. But I wouldn't do that anymore unless you plan to stop. More than once *is* a little creepy, Dylan."

I laugh a little. Mom has always been funny.

"Life's short, buddy," she says and sits next to me. She suddenly looks *so tired.* "We know that all too well. Things can change in the blink of an eye."

My parents never recovered from losing my brother—not that they *should.* But it's given them a different perspective on things. Sometimes, Mom reminds me of that.

"I can't force her to want something she doesn't, you know."

"But you don't know if she *does* because you didn't ask her. The worst she can say is no."

I sip my coffee again, contemplating.

She's right. I've been pretty miserable since Maddie got on that elevator.

Maybe I need to stop being so proud and just have a conversation with the woman. For fuck's sake, we're adults.

"Fine." I set the mug down and stand, looking for my keys. "I'll go see her."

"Attaboy," Mom says with a grin. "Go get your woman."

"She's not mine. Yet."

Maddie doesn't live too far from my parents', actually, just a few miles in a nearby neighborhood of North Seattle.

I checked.

The townhouse is nice and on the newer side. It's definitely in a safe part of town, which makes me feel better.

When I park near Maddie's unit, I have to take a minute to calm my nerves.

Showing up like this might annoy the hell out of her.

Shit, I'm annoyed at myself.

Finally, I step out of the car, walk to Maddie's door, and ring the bell. It's Saturday, so she shouldn't be in the office today.

Then again, she might have gone in to make up for being away over the holidays.

But within a minute of me ringing the doorbell, it opens, and Maddie's eyes widen and then blink fast when she sees me.

"Did I wish hard enough for you that I conjured you out of thin air?"

And just like that, all of my doubts disappear.

"I was in the neighborhood," I reply. I want to reach for her, pull her into my arms, and kiss the hell out of her.

But I wait.

"Come in," Maddie says and steps back. She brushes her hair away from her clean face. I realize that she's in shorts and a T-shirt with her hair up as if she's been exercising or working on a project.

"I'm sorry if I interrupted anything."

"You saved me," she says with a smile. "I was about to get started on painting the kitchen. It needs it, and I have the time these days."

"Why's that?"

"Oh, I quit my job."

I smile and offer my hand for a high-five. "Nice."

"It was overdue. When I went into the office on Monday, Jim was an asshat, and I decided it just wasn't worth it."

"I'm glad."

"What are you up to?"

I lick my lips and take in Maddie's home. It's exactly what I would have pictured for her: no clutter, clean lines on the furniture, pretty things on the walls.

"Well, I was just at my parents' house and decided to come over here to see you."

She frowns. "Your parents live in Seattle?"

"Yeah. Actually, Seattle is my home base when I'm not out on assignment."

She opens her mouth, then closes it again, scowling at me. "You never told me that."

"I guess it didn't come up."

"And all this time, I assumed you were from, like, New York or something."

"Nope. Seattle. And I know we said that Iceland was it for us, the whole vacation fling thing, but I kind of think that's ridiculous, Maddie."

"I do, too. Now."

"What?"

"I had no idea that you were in Seattle so often. I figured it would be impossible for us to see each other. And we never talked about it lasting past Iceland."

"We didn't talk enough about the important stuff." I shove my hand through my hair in frustration. "That needs to change immediately. I'll go first. Maddie, I'm completely in love with you. I don't know where this relationship is going, but I want to date you. I want to be with you every chance I get. I don't want to just walk away and never see you again. That's just torture for me."

A slow smile spreads over her beautiful face. "Same."

"To which part?"

"All of it. The dating, the being together." She steps to me and boosts herself onto her toes so she can press her lips to mine. "And the love thing. I'm sorry I didn't speak up in Iceland when I knew that I wanted more. I guess I was just scared that you'd say no."

"From now on, we speak up. No matter what."

I push her against the wall and kiss her like a starving man.

Because I *am* starving for her.

"Um, Dylan?"

"Yes, baby?"

"I *did* already paint this wall."

I pause and then grin against her mouth. "Well, then. I guess we're going to need a shower."

"Later." I lift her, my hands planted on her ass, and she wraps her legs around my waist. "Much later."

Epilogue

Caleb Montgomery

"They're on their way over," my wife informs me from the kitchen. "Turn that game off."

"No. If he can't handle a little football, he shouldn't be trying to worm his way into this family."

I can hear Brynna rolling her eyes from here. "Don't be difficult."

"She's my daughter. Being difficult is my one and only job in life."

I hear her stomping into the room from behind me. She grabs the remote out of my hand and turns off the TV.

"Hey!"

"Don't you *hey* me. Maddie is bringing a man here to meet us, and you're not going to be your usual grouchy, macho, alpha self about it."

"Yeah, Legs, I am. It's my right."

She just shakes her head and walks back into the kitchen.

"According to Josie, he's a *nice* guy. And he's part of the reason our daughter is laughing and a little outgoing again, Caleb. We haven't seen her like this in a long time, and I for one plan to thank him for it."

I know. I know this man who seems to have swept my girl off her feet in a foreign country is the reason she's so damn happy she radiates sunshine.

But, damn it, she's my daughter. I'm allowed to feel a certain way about it.

The doorbell rings, and Brynna hurries out of the kitchen to answer the door.

"Be nice," she hisses at me before opening it. "Hi, you two. Come on in. I hope you're hungry because I made a lot of food."

"I'm always hungry," comes a man's voice.

When they step inside, I can tell that I'm going to like him. Though he doesn't need to know that yet, of course.

I like that he has his hand on the small of Maddie's back. I like that he takes her coat and hangs it on the hook by the door before doing the same for himself.

I like that he looks at her with respect in his eyes.

"Mom, Dad, I want to introduce you to Dylan."

"It's a pleasure to meet you."

He shakes Brynna's hand and then walks over to me to do the same.

It's a good sign that he has a firm, confident handshake.

So far, there's nothing here for me to break his legs over.

Let's see if he can maintain that.

"Uh, I'm going to go help Mom in the kitchen," Maddie says, and after a supportive pat on Dylan's shoulder, she and Brynna walk away from us.

"Have a seat." I gesture to the couch opposite me, and we both sit. "You're from Seattle?"

"I am, yes." He goes on to talk about school, his parents, and his job. And when he gets to the part about meeting my daughter, his eyes light up.

"I have to thank you." My words seem to surprise us both. "Maddie has been...well, *different* for a long time. Not quite herself. But since she met you, she's quick to laugh. She seems *lighter*, as if a weight's been lifted off her shoulders. I have my daughter back."

"She was always there," he says, shaking his head.

"But, sometimes, a person comes into our lives and unlocks something we've had hidden away for a while. I know. It happened for me when I met Brynna."

Dylan sits forward, bracing his elbows on his knees. "I love your daughter. I know I haven't known her very long, but there's a connection between us that doesn't happen every day. I plan to build on that."

I nod, and the women return from the kitchen, cutting off any more private conversation between us.

Maddie sits next to Dylan, and his hand immediately lands on her knee.

I tense.

"Don't kill him," Brynna whispers to me. "We're having a nice evening."

"He's got his hands on her."

She smiles and kisses my cheek. "It's okay. But if he screws it all up, you can kill him then."

"Count on it."

* * * *

Also from 1001 Dark Nights and Kristen Proby, discover Change With Me, Shine With Me, Wonder With Me, Soaring With Fallon, Tempting Brooke, No Reservations, Easy With You, Easy For Keeps, and Indulge With Me.

Sign up for the 1001 Dark Nights Newsletter
and be entered to win a Tiffany Key necklace.

There's a contest every month!

Go to www.1001DarkNights.com to subscribe.

**As a bonus, all subscribers can download FIVE FREE exclusive
books!**

Discover 1001 Dark Nights Collection Nine

DRAGON UNBOUND by Donna Grant
A Dragon Kings Novella

NOTHING BUT INK by Carrie Ann Ryan
A Montgomery Ink: Fort Collins Novella

THE MASTERMIND by Dylan Allen
A Rivers Wilde Novella

JUST ONE WISH by Carly Phillips
A Kingston Family Novella

BEHIND CLOSED DOORS by Skye Warren
A Rochester Novella

GOSSAMER IN THE DARKNESS by Kristen Ashley
A Fantasyland Novella

DELIGHTED by Lexi Blake
A Masters and Mercenaries Novella

THE GRAVESIDE BAR AND GRILL by Darynda Jones
A Charley Davidson Novella

THE ANTI-FAN AND THE IDOL by Rachel Van Dyken
A My Summer In Seoul Novella

CHARMED BY YOU by J. Kenner
A Stark Security Novella

THE CLOSE-UP by Kennedy Ryan
A Hollywood Renaissance Novella

DESCEND TO DARKNESS by Heather Graham
A Krewe of Hunters Novella

BOND OF PASSION by Larissa Ione
A Demonica Novella

JUST WHAT I NEEDED by Kylie Scott
A Stage Dive Novella

THE SCRAMBLE by Kristen Proby
A Single in Seattle Novella

Also from Blue Box Press

THE BAIT by C.W. Gortner and M.J. Rose

THE FASHION ORPHANS by Randy Susan Meyers and M.J. Rose

TAKING THE LEAP by Kristen Ashley
A River Rain Novel

SAPPHIRE SUNSET by Christopher Rice writing as C. Travis Rice
A Sapphire Cove Novel

THE WAR OF TWO QUEENS by Jennifer L. Armentrout
A Blood and Ash Novel

THE MURDERS AT FLEAT HOUSE by Lucinda Riley

THE HEIST by C.W. Gortner and M.J. Rose

SAPPHIRE SPRING by Christopher Rice writing as C. Travis Rice
A Sapphire Cove Novel

MAKING THE MATCH by Kristen Ashley
A River Rain Novel

A LIGHT IN THE FLAME by Jennifer L. Armentrout
A Flesh and Fire Novel

Discover More Kristen Proby

Change With Me: A With Me In Seattle Novella

Zane Cooper. Hollywood royalty. Fourth generation superstar. He knows what it is to be one of the biggest celebrities in the world. And how lonely that title truly is. When scandal hits, his career hangs in the balance, and Zane flees LA for Seattle, laying low with his newly married best friend. Things will eventually blow over, and he'll have his life back soon enough.

Aubrey Stansfield arrives in Seattle excited to start a new job, and eager to settle into her new home. But when she arrives at her rental, Aubrey's sure she's imagining things because the uber sexy Zane Cooper is unpacking in *her* new bedroom. Thanks to a rental snafu, and unwilling to relocate on such short notice, Aubrey and Zane are thrust into being roommates.

Aubrey is about as average as a woman gets, so what could the megastar possibly see in her? She tells herself she's not interested, despite their undeniable chemistry. But Zane is very persuasive, and soon Aubrey finds herself playing house with the most recognized man on the planet. Deep down, she knows it's all a fantasy. He'll head back to his posh lifestyle soon and leave her behind. No way could she fall in love with him.

But love doesn't always follow the rules…

* * * *

Shine With Me: A With Me In Seattle Novella

Sabrina Harrison *hates* being famous. She walked away from show business, from the flashing bulbs and prying eyes years ago, and is happy in her rural Oregon home, dedicating her life to her non-profit.

Until Hollywood calls, offering her the role of a lifetime. In more than ten years, she's never felt the pull to return to the business that shunned her, but this role is everything Sabrina's ever longed for.

Now she has to get in shape for it.

Benjamin Demarco's gym, Sound Fitness, continues making a name for itself in Seattle. And now, he finds himself with the task of training Sabrina, getting her in shape for the role of her life. He's trained hundreds of women. This is his job. So why does he suddenly see Sabrina as more than just another client? His hands linger on her skin, his breath catches when she's near.

He knows better. Soon, she'll be gone, living her life. A life that doesn't include him.

* * * *

Wonder With Me: With Me In Seattle Novella

Reed Taylor doesn't pay much attention to the holidays—until he receives a surprise present. Four-year-old Piper is the daughter he never knew about, and with the death of her mother, is also now the roommate he never expected. He's determined to make their first Christmas together one she'll never forget.

Noel Thompson has gotten her share of strange requests in her career as an interior designer. The call to design a beautiful home for Christmas is more like a dream come true. And that was *before* she met her new employer—sexy and mysterious, he's everything she ever hoped Santa would bring her.

As Noel showers his home with holiday spirit, Reed showers Piper with love. And the busy life he's created for himself no longer seems nearly as important as the one Noel is helping him build with his daughter. But if he can't convince his decorator to stay, this could be the only year he feels the true wonder of the season.

Tempting Brooke: A Big Sky Novella

Brooke's Blooms has taken Cunningham Falls by surprise. The beautiful, innovative flower shop is trendy, with not only gorgeous flower arrangements, but also fun gifts for any occasion. This store is Brooke Henderson's deepest joy, and it means everything to her, which shows in how completely she and her little shop have been embraced by the small community of Cunningham Falls.

So, when her landlord dies and Brody Chabot saunters through her door, announcing that the building has been sold, and will soon be demolished, Brooke knows that she's in for the fight of her life. But she hasn't gotten this far by sitting back and quietly doing what she's told. *Hustle* is Brooke's middle name, and she has no intention of losing this fight, no matter how tempting Brody's smile -- and body - is.

No Reservations: A Fusion Novella

Chase MacKenzie is *not* the man for Maura Jenkins. A self proclaimed life-long bachelor, and unapologetic about his distaste for monogamy, a woman would have to be a masochist to want to fall into Chase's bed.

And Maura is no masochist.

Chase has one strict rule: no strings attached. Which is fine with Maura because she doesn't even really *like* Chase. He's arrogant, cocky and let's not forget bossy. But when he aims that crooked grin at her she goes weak in the knees. Not that she has any intentions of falling for his charms.

Definitely not.

Well, maybe just once…

Easy For Keeps: A Boudreaux Novella

Adam Spencer loves women. All women. Every shape and size, regardless of hair or eye color, religion or race, he simply enjoys them all. Meeting more than his fair share as the manager and head bartender of The Odyssey, a hot spot in the heart of New Orleans' French Quarter, Adam's comfortable with his lifestyle, and sees no reason to change it. A wife and kids, plus the white picket fence are not in the cards for this confirmed bachelor. Until a beautiful woman, and her sweet princess, literally knock him on his ass.

Sarah Cox has just moved to New Orleans, having accepted a position as a social worker specializing in at-risk women and children. It's a demanding, sometimes dangerous job, but Sarah is no shy wallflower. She can handle just about anything that comes at her, even the attentions of one sexy Adam Spencer. Just because he's charmed her daughter, making her think of magical kingdoms with happily ever after, doesn't mean that Sarah believes in fairy tales. But the more time she spends with the enchanting man, the more he begins to sway her into believing in forever.

Even so, when Sarah's job becomes more dangerous than any of them bargained for, will she be ripped from Adam's life forever?

* * * *

Easy With You: A With You In Seattle Novella

Nothing has ever come easy for Lila Bailey. She's fought for every good thing in her life during every day of her thirty-one years. Aside from that one night with an impossible to deny stranger a year ago, Lila is the epitome of responsible.

Steadfast. Strong.

She's pulled herself out of the train wreck of her childhood, proud to be a professor at Tulane University and laying down roots in a city she's grown to love. But when some of her female students are viciously murdered, Lila's shaken to the core and unsure of whom she can trust in New Orleans. When the police detective assigned to the murder case comes to investigate, she's even more surprised to find herself staring into the eyes of the man that made her toes curl last year.

In an attempt to move on from the tragic loss of his wife, Asher Smith moved his daughter and himself to a new city, ready for a fresh start. A damn fine police lieutenant, but new to the New Orleans force, Asher has a lot to prove to his colleagues and himself.

With a murderer terrorizing the Tulane University campus, Asher finds himself toe-to-toe with the one woman that haunts his dreams. His hands, his lips, his body know her as intimately as he's ever known anyone. As he learns her mind and heart as well, Asher wants nothing more than to keep her safe, in his bed, and in his and his daughter's lives for the long haul.

But when Lila becomes the target, can Asher save her in time, or will he lose another woman he loves?

* * * *

Soaring with Fallon: A Big Sky Novel

Fallon McCarthy has climbed the corporate ladder. She's had the office with the view, the staff, and the plaque on her door. The unexpected loss of her grandmother taught her that there's more to life than meetings and conference calls, so she quit, and is happy to be a nomad, checking off items on her bucket list as she takes jobs teaching yoga in each place she lands in. She's happy being free, and has no interest in being tied down.

When Noah King gets the call that an eagle has been injured, he's not expecting to find a beautiful stranger standing vigil when he arrives. Rehabilitating birds of prey is Noah's passion, it's what he lives for, and he doesn't have time for a nosy woman who's suddenly taken an interest in Spread Your Wings sanctuary.

But Fallon's gentle nature, and the way she makes him laugh, and *feel* again draws him in. When it comes time for Fallon to move on, will Noah's love be enough for her to stay, or will he have to find the strength to let her fly?

* * * *

Indulge With Me: A With Me In Seattle Celebration
Short stories by Kristen Proby
Recipes from Suzanne M. Johnson

The beloved Montgomery Family, from New York Times Bestselling author Kristen Proby's With Me In Seattle series, is big, and it just keeps growing! There are parties and celebrations taking place at every turn, and we are delighted to invite you to all of the festivities!

Whether it's a brunch hosted by Nate and Jules McKenna, or a fancy dinner party hosted by Luke and Natalie Williams, you won't want to miss all we have in store for you! Each all-new story will feature shenanigans, laughter, love and lots of food.

And let's not forget cocktails!

Kristen, along with USA Today Bestselling author Suzanne Johnson, have teamed up to bring you this cookbook, celebrating family, love, and absolutely delicious foods, perfect for any occasion.

So sit back, or march straight into the kitchen, and get ready to indulge. We hope you're hungry!

The Secret
Single in Seattle, Book 1
By Kristen Proby
Now Available!

If you are new to the Single in Seattle series, I'd love to introduce you to the first in the series, The Secret, featuring Olivia and Vaughn!

Here is a little sneak peek:

I walk through the door to my office and come to an abrupt stop.

Sitting *on my freaking desk*, his feet dangling, is Vaughn Barrymore. He scowls when he sees me in the doorway.

"You know, you could have let me know that you were going to be late," he says.

I blink, walk inside, and shut the door, setting the folders and papers in my arms on a shelf before propping my hands on my hips.

"I'm Olivia Conner. I'll be working with you. Of course, our appointment was scheduled for *yesterday,* and you didn't call to reschedule, but I'll make room in *my* busy schedule to fit you in. You're welcome."

That scowl doesn't leave his too-handsome-for-his-own-good face. "We did not have an appointment yesterday. It's today."

"Yesterday," I repeat and reach for my measuring tape, trying to ignore the fact that Vaughn might be sexier in person than he is in the movies. "But we can knock it out right now before my next appointment. It won't take long. Just stand over here."

Vaughn hops off the desk and stands in the middle of the room. I squat before him, tape in hand to measure his inseam, then frown.

"You're wearing jeans."

"Smart one, aren't you?"

I raise my eyebrows and stare up at him. God, he *is* hotter in person. That's just not fair.

Get it together, Liv. You're a professional.

"I asked you to wear sweats or something loose so I could get an accurate measurement. It's important."

Without a word, Vaughn takes off his shoes, unfastens his jeans, lets them drop to pool around his feet, then steps out of them and flicks them aside with his toe.

Thank God he's wearing underwear.

I mean, it's tight-as-hell boxer briefs and leaves absolutely *nothing* to the imagination, but he's covered.

Sort of.

And holy Jesus in Heaven, the man is *hung*. How am I going to get this measurement without making a fool of myself?

"Better?"

"Sure. Just...spread your legs a bit."

He grins and obliges.

"This isn't so bad, after all," he says, and I snarl at him.

He's warm and so freaking *firm* as I measure from his crotch to his ankle and then quickly move to his waist, turning to jot down the numbers.

I have to measure each thigh and calf, and then, finally, I can stand before him and out of range of *that*.

God, I'm flushed. Sure, Vaughn's potent on screen, but he's no less so in person. Maybe even *sexier* in person. I wasn't expecting that.

He's also cocky and rude.

"Please raise your arms like this." I lift mine straight out from my sides, and he mimics me. "Perfect."

I have to wrap my arms around him, like in a hug, to grab the tape and pull it around his chest. When I lean in, I swear I hear him take a deep breath through his nose, near my head.

"Did you just *sniff* me?" I demand after jerking back.

His lips—his *full* and gorgeous lips—twist into a sneer. "In your dreams, sweetheart."

About Kristen Proby

New York Times and *USA Today* bestselling author Kristen Proby has published more than sixty romance novels. She is best known for her self-published With Me In Seattle and Boudreaux series. Kristen lives in Montana with her husband, two cats, and a spoiled dog.

Discover 1001 Dark Nights

TO SERVE by Laura Kaye ~ DRAGON FEVER by Donna Grant ~ KAYDEN/SIMON by Alexandra Ivy/Laura Wright ~ STRUNG UP by Lorelei James ~ MIDNIGHT UNTAMED by Lara Adrian ~ TRICKED by Rebecca Zanetti ~ DIRTY WICKED by Shayla Black ~ THE ONLY ONE by Lauren Blakely ~ SWEET SURRENDER by Liliana Hart

COLLECTION FOUR
ROCK CHICK REAWAKENING by Kristen Ashley ~ ADORING INK by Carrie Ann Ryan ~ SWEET RIVALRY by K. Bromberg ~ SHADE'S LADY by Joanna Wylde ~ RAZR by Larissa Ione ~ ARRANGED by Lexi Blake ~ TANGLED by Rebecca Zanetti ~ HOLD ME by J. Kenner ~ SOMEHOW, SOME WAY by Jennifer Probst ~ TOO CLOSE TO CALL by Tessa Bailey ~ HUNTED by Elisabeth Naughton ~ EYES ON YOU by Laura Kaye ~ BLADE by Alexandra Ivy/Laura Wright ~ DRAGON BURN by Donna Grant ~ TRIPPED OUT by Lorelei James ~ STUD FINDER by Lauren Blakely ~ MIDNIGHT UNLEASHED by Lara Adrian ~ HALLOW BE THE HAUNT by Heather Graham ~ DIRTY FILTHY FIX by Laurelin Paige ~ THE BED MATE by Kendall Ryan ~ NIGHT GAMES by CD Reiss ~ NO RESERVATIONS by Kristen Proby ~ DAWN OF SURRENDER by Liliana Hart

COLLECTION FIVE
BLAZE ERUPTING by Rebecca Zanetti ~ ROUGH RIDE by Kristen Ashley ~ HAWKYN by Larissa Ione ~ RIDE DIRTY by Laura Kaye ~ ROME'S CHANCE by Joanna Wylde ~ THE MARRIAGE ARRANGEMENT by Jennifer Probst ~ SURRENDE by Elisabeth Naughton ~ INKED NIGHTS by Carrie Ann Ryan ~ ENVY by Rachel Van Dyken ~ PROTECTED by Lexi Blake ~ THI PRINCE by Jennifer L. Armentrout ~ PLEASE ME by J. Kenner ~ WOUND TIGHT by Lorelei James ~ STRONG by Kylie Scott ~ DRAGON NIGHT by Donna Grant ~ TEMPTING BROOKE by Kristen Proby ~ HAUNTED BE THE HOLIDAYS by Heather Graham ~ CONTROL by K. Bromberg ~ HUNKY

HEARTBREAKER by Kendall Ryan ~ THE DARKEST CAPTIVE by Gena Showalter

WIND by Kristen Ashley ~ DARE TO TEASE by Carly Phillips ~
VAMPIRE by Rebecca Zanetti ~ MAFIA KING by Rachel Van
Dyken ~ THE GRAVEDIGGER'S SON by Darynda Jones ~
FINALE by Skye Warren ~ MEMORIES OF YOU by J. Kenner ~
SLAYED BY DARKNESS by Alexandra Ivy ~ TREASURED by L
Blake ~ THE DAREDEVIL by Dylan Allen ~ BOND OF DESTIN
by Larissa Ione ~ MORE THAN POSSESS YOU by Shayla Black
HAUNTED HOUSE by Heather Graham ~ MAN FOR ME by
Laurelin Paige ~ THE RHYTHM METHOD by Kylie Scott ~
JONAH BENNETT by Tijan ~ CHANGE WITH ME by Krister
Proby ~ THE DARKEST DESTINY by Gena Showalter

Discover Blue Box Press
TAME ME by J. Kenner ~ TEMPT ME by J. Kenner ~ DAMIEN I
J. Kenner ~ TEASE ME by J. Kenner ~ REAPER by Larissa Ione
THE SURRENDER GATE by Christopher Rice ~ SERVICING TH
TARGET by Cherise Sinclair ~ THE LAKE OF LEARNING by Ste
Berry and M.J. Rose ~ THE MUSEUM OF MYSTERIES by Steve
Berry and M.J. Rose ~ TEASE ME by J. Kenner ~ FROM BLOOL
AND ASH by Jennifer L. Armentrout ~ QUEEN MOVE by Kenne
Ryan ~ THE HOUSE OF LONG AGO by Steve Berry and M.J. Ro
~ THE BUTTERFLY ROOM by Lucinda Riley ~ A KINGDOM C
FLESH AND FIRE by Jennifer L. Armentrout ~ THE LAST TIAR
by M.J. Rose ~ THE CROWN OF GILDED BONES by Jennifer I
Armentrout ~ THE MISSING SISTER by Lucinda Riley ~ THE EN
OF FOREVER by Steve Berry and M.J. Rose ~ THE STEAL by C. V
Gortner and M.J. Rose ~ CHASING SERENITY by Kristen Ashley
A SHADOW IN THE EMBER by Jennifer L. Armentrout

On Behalf of 1001 Dark Nights,

Liz Berry, M.J. Rose, and Jillian Stein would like to thank ~

Steve Berry
Doug Scofield
Benjamin Stein
Kim Guidroz
Social Butterfly PR
Asha Hossain
Chris Graham
Chelle Olson
Kasi Alexander
Jessica Saunders
Dylan Stockton
Kate Boggs
Richard Blake
and Simon Lipskar

Made in the USA
Las Vegas, NV
29 November 2022

60632960R00062